THE REAL DOPEBOYZ OF ATLANTA 2

A STREET LOVE TALE

SHAN

SUBMIT/SUBSCRIBE

Text Shanbooks to 22828 to stay up to date with new releases, sneak peeks, contest, and more...

Shan Presents is currently accepting submissions in Urban Fiction, African American Romance, AA Criminal Romance, and Street Lit, Women's/Contemporary Fiction...

If you have a finished manuscript that you would like to send for consideration, please send the following to submissions@shanpresents.com

1)Contact information

2)Synopsis

3)First 3 chapters in a Word DOC

If Shan Presents has any interest in your work, the full novel will be requested.

PREVIOUSLY IN THE REAL DOPEBOYZ OF ATLANTA 1

Poetic

Tears rushed down my face as I drove down the long driveway that led to my parents' home. My entire body was shaking, and it felt like I had driven the entire way there in a daze. My heart thumped erratically against my chest, and when I finally reached the end of the driveway and placed the car in park, I took in a deep breath and tugged at the Poetic necklace that dangled at the center of my chest.

I thought about trying Ahmeen again, but I had already called him four times on the way here and not once had he answered. Shaking my head, I rubbed the tears from my face and veered out my front window. The contents in my stomach felt like they were going to come up, when I looked up and spotted Chuck helping Lyric out of her car and into the house.

My forehead wrinkled in confusion, and I pushed the car to the door open and slowly stepped out. Nausea took over and forced me to kneel over and throw up everything that I had left in me. Coughing, I pulled my hair from my face and then gathered myself before going inside of the home.

"I don't know what's gotten into her," I heard Lyric's cries the moment I walked in, and something told me to just walk out of the door, but I couldn't.

I followed where I heard her voice coming from and just stood in the doorway, but didn't say anything. My father, mother, Chuck, Tyree, Maino were all sitting in our family room with all eyes on Lyric. Her hair was all over her head. She had a bruise under her eye, and specks of blood near what looked like a busted a lip.

I frowned, not knowing what the fuck was going on. I knew for a fact that when I left that apartment after going to get my necklace that I left behind that Lyric was fine. She didn't have a fucking mark on her. I knew she was fine because after I had heard Steve admit that Lyric had hired him to kill me and Loop, and that Melody had been in the wrong place at the wrong time, I saw her stab him two times, before I snatched my necklace up and left before she saw me. I sat in the parking lot of the car crying my eyes out and did everything I could to get myself together so that I could drive here. I never in a million years imagined that I would only come home to this.

"Steve just kept saying that Poe had Melody killed and that she had conspired with the Shakur brothers to make it happen. He said he was there for the rest of the payment she owed him, and when I told him that I was calling Chuck, he attacked me. That's when I stabbed him to get him off of me, but I didn't think that I was going to kill him," Lyric cried, putting on an award winning show. If I hadn't witnessed everything myself then I would've thought that she was serious.

"So all this time she been fucking with that nigga and more than likely giving him the drop on everything we had going on," my pops said, shaking his head like he was very disappointed in me.

"If you could've seen all those pictures that bitch Eve had. Picture after picture of them together. She been fucking this nigga for a long ass time. Nigga talking about squashing a beef. Fuck that," Maino spat.

"Remember I told you baby I saw her standing outside the game room that day listening to you and Maino's conversation. That was the same day I saw that hickey on her neck that you swore up and down wasn't one. So she had my fuckin' baby killed. Wow," my mama chimed in and suddenly started crying. "That little bitch been playing us all along."

"She gave them Quavo, too! She told them that he killed their mama. I can show you the Instagram message that he showed me that was sent from her to this dude name Dez that works for the Shakur family," Lyric said, and that time I scoffed so loudly that everybody turned around and looked at me.

"Poe...come here," my father urged as he stood up from the couch and turned around to face me.

I shook my head and backed away. Grabbing my cell phone from out of my pocket, I rushed to unlock it and tried to call Ahmeen again. My hands trembled as my father started to walk around the couch towards me. He had a look so cold in his eyes that I couldn't find an ounce of love left for me.

"Poe..." Maino said next as I continued to back away.

"Don't you walk out that door," my father said, and when he moved quicker towards me, I turned around and took off running.

"Ahmeeennnnn!" I screamed once I had made it outside and raced towards my car.

Ahmeen had finally answered my call, but the only thing I heard was what was sounded like someone gasping for air.

"Ahmeen?" I questioned, and looked down at my phone. Seeing that he hadn't hung up, I placed the phone back to my ear. "Ahmeen! Ahmeeeen!"

"Ca...ca...ca call...an am...ambulance," I heard him gurgle.

1

POETIC

"Ahmeen?" I questioned and looked down at my phone. Seeing that he hadn't hung up, I placed the phone back to my ear. "Ahmeen! Ahmeeeen!"

"Ca...ca...ca call...an am...ambulance," I heard him gurgle.

"Oh, my God, baby! Ahmeen!" I yelled again, but the line went dead.

My mind was all over the place. I stood frozen trying to figure out what was going on around me. My sister had just turned everything on me and my family had believed her. That was the least of my worries though. It seemed like Ahmeen was in need of help, and when I remembered how messed up he'd just sounded, I'd snapped out of it.

I dropped my phone into my purse and replaced it with my gun. Spinning around, I quickly removed the safety and pointed it at my father and brother Maino, who were coming for me. My heart pounded against my chest, and I sucked my teeth knowing that, with the way I felt right now, I would drop either of them if they came at me.

"What the fuck?" Maino was the first to say as his mouth dropped while he stared at me.

"Poe...are you fuckin' crazy?" my dad asked, and I shook my head as tears spilled down my face.

"Get the fuck away from me!" I told them, my hand shaking as I kept the gun pointed at them.

I took one hand away from the gun, leaving it pointed in their direction and then went back into my purse for my phone. Backing away towards my car, I dialed 911 and waited for the operator to pick up.

"Poe!" my father yelled, and when I thought he was going to lunge at me, I pulled the trigger.

My mouth dropped open, and when I realized that I had missed and hadn't hit anyone, I quickly got into my car, and placed the gun on the center console. Quickly cranking the engine, I pushed the car in reverse and backed out so fast that I almost ran into the gate that surrounded our house.

"...hello, is anyone there? Hello!" I heard someone say.

"Oh, shit...Hello! I need to get help for my boyfriend. I'm not sure what's going on, but he sounded like he was having a hard time breathing."

"Ma'am, what is your name?" the operator asked as I pulled through the gate and sped off into the street.

"Poetic King," I told her, glaring in my rearview mirror. "Please, his address is...it's 1805 Ferncliff Rd. Please send him help!"

"Do you know if he has been injured. Is he currently breathing?"

"Ma'am, I am not there. I called him, and he told me to call an ambulance. Can you please send someone? It's going to take me at least twenty minutes to get to him," I yelled into the phone. "Just send someone!"

"Help is on the way ma'am. Please call us back if you need anything."

I hung the phone up and tried to call Ahmeen back. I didn't know what was going on. When I had left him, I told him that I was coming right back. When I realized that I had left my necklace tucked underneath my mattress, he'd made me feel so bad about being so careless with it. He said that I acted like I didn't like or appreciate his gift but that wasn't the case at all. I loved that necklace and wore it every chance that I got. I just knew that if my parents ever saw it, they were going to wonder where I had gotten the money from. Yea, they gave me and my siblings money, but never enough for us to blow a bag such as the one that Ahmeen had. I had swore that when I got the necklace from the apartment that I was going to forever wear it and never take it off.

Ahmeen had insisted on going with me, but I was still hesitant and trying to hide our relationship in a way. He could sense it, and he was angry with me, and knowing that something might have happened to him while I was gone, was tearing me up inside. I didn't even care about what Lyric had done anymore. All I wanted was to get to my man and make sure that he was okay.

Tears clouded my vision as I drove as fast as I could towards my new home. My heartrate seemed to weaken the closer I got, and then beat uncontrollably with the thought of Ahmeen being dead when I arrived. I didn't know what I would do if I was to lose him. He was all I had at this point...well all me and our baby had.

He just gotta be okay; I thought to myself as I tried my hardest to just focus on the road.

Fifteen minutes later, I was pulling down the long road that led to the home I now shared with Ahmeen. Right ahead of me, I could see the ambulance driving quickly towards the house. I grimaced seeing that they were just now getting here. I smashed down on the gas, pushing the speed to almost 60, and causing the dirt road to make a cloud around me.

"Oh, my God, hurry up, hurry up!" I urged, just as I had caught up to the ambulance.

The location where Ahmeen had purchased this house was confusing. It was ducked off and you had to go down a long ass dirt road before you got to what looked like a forest of trees. It wasn't until you passed the trees that you saw the huge, beautiful home. I guess I shouldn't have been surprised that the ambulance was just now arriving. They had probably passed the entrance several times before figuring out where it was.

I pulled in right behind them and was so eager to get out that I had almost forgot to place the car in park. I hopped out and rushed down the sidewalk. It was blood everywhere, and the sight of it caused me to become sick to my stomach. Everything around me seemed to go in slow motion as I looked around for Ahmeen.

"Over here, over here!" I heard one of the EMTs yell, causing me to snap out of my daze.

Out the corner of my eye, I spotted Ahmeen, slumped over with his back against the sofa. The blood that covered his face caused me to rush towards him, pushing the EMTs out of the way in the process. His chest was barely moving and through the blood I could see that his eyes were closed.

"Ahmeen, baby, Meen. Please be okay! Talk to me," I seemed to say all in one breath.

"Excuse us ma'am!" the first EMT pushed as he swiftly began to cut away at Ahmeen's clothing.

"Call it in!" the second EMT yelled. "We have a gunshot victim. Looks like about one...two....oh, God. Three shots to the cranium!"

"Another shot right here...left chest area," the first EMT called out, my eyes burning with fear.

"Please save him. Please. Please. Please. Please, don't let him die," I mumbled, desperately holding onto Ahmeen's hand.

"Poe..." Meen coughed weakly.

"Meen!" I screamed, my eyes wide when he glared at me.

"My pops...call hi...him. Tell him...it...wa...Moni," Ahmeen got out before blood trickled down the side of his mouth and his head fell limp towards the side.

"Moni? Moni did this?"

2

DE'MONI

My chest heaved up and down and several times I tried to talk myself out of it. I guess muh'fuckas could say that I had truly lost my shit. That bitch Ayesha had really set a nigga up, and I couldn't even begin to understand the reason behind it. I had never met that broad a day in my life before I ran into her at the club that night. It was obvious she had it out for me and because of her, I committed the ultimate betrayal.

I wasn't even the type of nigga that would even do shit like this, but damn, my back was up against the wall. After Chanel told me she was pregnant, I started to panic. I wasn't even ready for a kid, but I really did love that girl and wanted to be there for her and my lil' one. It wasn't even the same feeling that I got when Ayesha claimed she was pregnant with my kid. I had felt some type of love I never felt before with Chanel. I was really tryna make shit right and be somewhat of a stand-up guy.

After me and Chanel celebrated her birthday that night, I went down to the police station along with my lawyer the next day. The type of time I was facing was enough for me to go home and put a bullet in my head. The case against me was solid and according to my lawyer, it was in my best interest to take whatever deal they had for me. I did what the fuck I had to do. I wasn't who they wanted for real, for real. Let them tell it, I was at the bottom of the barrel, and they really was after the big fish. They wanted the person who had been supplying all of Atlanta with this new, deadly strain of heroin. They had most of the puzzle pieces and was missing the main one...Ahmeen.

"Fuck...fuck....fuck. Shit," I chanted, desperately trying to get my nerves together. I took in a deep breath and just did it.

POW!

"Arrghhhhhhh!" I grunted, after shooting myself in my right leg.

I squinted my eyes closed before I sat back in the seat and allowed the pain I felt to travel through my body. Taking in deep breaths, and letting them all out, I opened my eyes and looked around. I was sitting in a park about five miles away from my pops' place. I knew that Ahmeen was dead and that I was going to have to explain this shit to them somehow. It wasn't nothing I could do to dismiss it and even act like I ain't know because I had just told Goat before I had pulled up on Ahmeen where I was and what I was doing there.

"Shit...one more..." I said, before placing my hand on the steering wheel.

POW!

The pain that ripped through my body caused every part of me to start shaking. I took a minute to get myself together before I again looked around to make sure that no one had saw me. It was dark as fuck and almost one in the morning. It seemed like out of nowhere, the sky filled with dark clouds that caused thunder to roar through the air.

"Fuck man..." I grunted while shaking my head.

I finally pulled out of the lot and headed towards my pops' house. The way there seemed to be long and part of me wanted to just go home, get Chanel, and blow this bitch, but I knew I couldn't. My freedom solely depended on me giving up Ahmeen and everything I knew about the drug organization that he had going on. Even with him dead or alive, all I had to do was prove that he was the supplier, and I walked away with full immunity.

They would only have me testify if the case went to trial, and they had promised me that they would allow me to remain anonymous in the event that it came to that. Me running would only look suspicious.

After a dreadful ten minute drive, I pulled up to my pops' house and started with the dramatics. I pushed the door open and fell down onto the pavement. I knew that my pops had cameras everywhere and the moment someone entered the property, every light surrounding the home popped on and the surveillance began recording.

"Pops!" I cried, as I limped towards the home.

My leg drug behind me as the blood that dripped from it decorated the driveway. Tears poured from my eyes, because I really did feel fucked up inside. I didn't want to have to kill Ahmeen, but he had really given me no other choice. He tried to treat me like I was some pussy so I had to show him who he was fucking with. Blood against blood, I was always going to choose myself.

"Pops..." I said, looking up at him once he appeared on the top of the stairs that led to his home. "It was Meen...he tried to kill me, and I ain't have no choice."

"Oh yea..." my pops told me, his tone unconvincing as he slid his phone into his pocket and jogged down the stairs.

I stopped moving once I spotted the rain of men with guns that suddenly appeared and followed behind him. It wasn't out of the ordinary that my pops would have men with him, but it was rare that he would have this many. Immediately, I felt like something wasn't right and backed up to where my car was parked.

"Where you going?" he asked me. "You bitch ass little nigga!"

I reached behind me and quickly pulled out my burner. I knew I was taking a big ass risk and that if I wasn't careful, I would have an army of bullets flying at me left and right.

"Back the fuck up!" I told him, and he held his hand up to let his men know not to move.

"You really done lost your fuckin' mind!" he yelled and I nodded.

"Just looking out for myself. I knew if it came down to it, you would have Ahmeen's back over mine!" I told him and pulled my car door open.

"Nigga have your back over his for what? You really did this shit, Moni? You really tried to kill your own brother?"

Tried? I thought to myself as a lump suddenly formed in my throat.

"Damn..." my pops chuckled as he rubbed the hairs on his beard. "You one fucked up ass nigga, son. I don't know where me and your mama went wrong with you, but just know you dead to me! You ain't shit to me no more lil' nigga."

"Nigga, I never was anything to you!" I yelled and rushed inside of the car.

I slammed the door shut and sped around the circular drive-way. I kept my head low in case they tried to pop me before I made it away from here. Looks like I ain't have no choice now but to go to Plan B... whatever the fuck that was.

When I made it back to my house, Chanel was running at me with a panicked look on her face. Whatever the fuck had happened had her so scared she didn't even notice the fact that I was covered in blood. Her arms went around me and she hugged me tightly before placing kisses on my face.

"Babbbbby, where were you? I was so scared," she said, pulling away and finally noticing my appearance. "Oh, my God, are you okay?"

"We gotta get the fuck up outta here," I told her, slightly pushing her to the side and moving towards the bedroom as fast as I could.

"Moni, please tell me what happened? Muthafuckas came rushing up in here and looking all over the place for you. Talking about you shot Ahmeen and that you were dead for it. What happened?" Chanel ranted and I sighed.

"How long ago was that?" I asked her and grimaced at the pain in my leg.

I grabbed a shirt from the dresser drawer and went over to the bed to sit down. I tried wrapping the towel around my leg when Chanel rushed over to me and took the towel from me. She used her strength to tear it up and then rolled my pants leg up. I watched how she flinched at the sight of the blood that oozed from the wound before she took the shirt and tied it as tightly as she could around my leg. My hand didn't even hurt as bad. The shit was numb and I was starting to think that I had lost feeling.

"How long ago did they come by here, Chanel?" I asked again.

"Like about maybe forty-five minutes ago..."

"Damn, so before I went there. Bet, we gotta go," I told her, and she sucked her teeth as tears started to fall down her face.

"Did you do that shit, Moni?"

"Chanel...you either riding with me or you riding with them. I don't got time to discuss shit. That nigga wanted me dead...you see this shit!" I yelled causing her to jump back. "I defended myself and because that nigga is worth more money to them, they rather me be dead. Now look, either you gonna be down for your nigga or not?"

"You know I'm with you through whatever. I'm just scared. We got a baby on the way, Moni," Chanel cried, and I stood up and pulled her in my arms.

"I know. And I know I been fucking up like crazy, but when we get this, just know I'mma make it all up to you, and our kid. That's my word," I promised her meaning every word.

"I know you will. I love you," Chanel told me.

"I love you too," I said for the first time ever.

Tears streamed down Chanel's face like a running faucet, and I held onto her for a long while. Shit like this made me regret every moment I had ever treated her dirty. She was a real one, and I was glad that I had her by my side cause a nigga had fucked up bad. I wasn't no Jay and Chanel wasn't no Bey, but we were about to be On the Run, and I couldn't even say if we could ever come back.

3

AHMEEN

Days Later...

"Aye, get me the fuck up out of here!" I shot up, before I gripped my stomach and started coughing.

My eyes felt heavy as I looked around and blinked rapidly trying to see who was around me. When I narrowed in on Poe sitting in a chair right next to me with her eyes wide with fear, I calmed down a little, but then I remembered what happened to me.

My breathing was suddenly rapid and caused the machines that were connected to my body to beep out of control. I gritted down on my teeth as I sat forward prepared to get out this muthafucka. The only thing that was on my mind was revenge, and I wanted it bad. Brother or not, that nigga was gon' catch hell the moment I stepped foot back on the pavement.

I patted my body down, feeling the bandages that was practically covering my entire stomach, and then brought my hand up to my head. Pain shot through every part of my body causing me to be even angrier. The same way my head was at Moni's feet when he pumped those last three bullets in me, I wanted him in the same fuckin' position, only I wasn't going to fuck it up.

This dude had really turned state on a nigga. He had given the DA everything they needed to know about me, and what I did when it came to this heroin. They knew that I was the one that had developed the new recipe that had even the elite of Atlanta hooked. Moni had told them that I was the nigga to see—the supplier, the plug, the connect. Only thing that was working in my favor was that he had told them and yet to provide any concrete info. It was my word against his. I didn't even know exactly how I wanted to play this shit, but I knew that I wanted him dead for what he had done to me.

"Son...son, calm down," my pops lulled, and I shook my head and began snatching cords away from me.

"Nah...get me the fuck outta here. Take me to my house. It's too open in here," I told him, and he shook his head just as the staff from the hospital rushed into the room.

"We got the building surrounded. It's three of our men outside the door and more throughout the hospital..."

"I don't care about any of that. I'm ready to go home."

"Mr. Shakur. There is still a bullet in the middle of your stomach. Too much movement and it can shift and possibly cause much more damage than it already has. I told you that we needed to give it some time before we figure out our next steps. You resting, and allowing your body to heal is imperative to your recovery," the doctor said, and I shook my head not giving a fuck what he was talking about.

"Get me a hospital bed at home. You come to me..."

"I don't operate like..."

"Doctor, let me speak with you outside," my pops interjected, and I shook my head and sat forward when the two of them walked out.

"You're really about to leave?" Poe asked me, her lips curled into a frown as she eyed me.

"I'm getting the fuck up outta here," I told her and reached over to my side to let the railing down.

"Are you fucking stupid? You just suffered from four damn gunshot wounds...three to your damn head and you're trying to leave like this shit is normal and happens every day?"

"Nothing about my life is normal, but you crazy if you think

I'mma sit here like a sitting duck waiting for a nigga to try and touch me again," I spat and gripped at my side when excruciating pains shot through me.

"Ahmeen!" Poe yelled before rushing to the other side of the bed.

She grabbed my arm, and I used her shoulder to help me stand completely up. Tears stung the corner of my eyes as every part of my body suddenly felt like it was on fire. I tried to push through it and take a step, only causing myself to go crashing to the floor taking the IV pole, and the tray that was next to my bedside along with me.

My damn head started to spin like crazy as Poe and a couple of the nurses scurried to help me up from the floor. A nigga wanted to cry like a bitch seeing that I was in no condition to do shit but lay on my back. Moni had really done a number on me, but I swore on everything I was going to bounce back. I was too thorough and real for this shit.

"Excuse me, Ahmeen Shakur..."

The moment I was placed back into the hospital bed, I looked up to see two dudes in suits standing in the doorway. It took only a second for the me to notice the silver badges that hung around their necks and recognize that they were police. I figured they were here to ask questions about my shooting, but when I saw the way my pops looked as he stood on the outside of the door, unable to come back into the room, I knew something was up.

"I'm Detective Calloway, and this is my partner Detective Fisher," the tall, Black guy that was rocking a gray button up and brown slacks said as he stared at me like we had beef.

"Sup..." I grunted, scowling from the pain that seemed to affect my damn soul.

"We're here to serve a warrant for your arrest on the murder of Quavarious Childs," the other one, a short, White guy with a scruffy beard said.

"What?" Poetic questioned, and I sucked my teeth. "He ain't murdered no damn body! Someone tried to fuckin' kill him and you bring your asses down here to accuse him of some shit! What kinda bullshit is this?"

"Chill..." I tried to tell Poe, but she wasn't going.

"No, fuck that. Y'all need to be out here trying to find the person that did this to him! Look at him! He almost died!" she yelled, before tears shot from her eyes like a burst of raindrops.

"Escort her out of her eplease. Because the doctor has informed us that you are not able to leave here, we will hold you here in the custody of the Atlanta Police Department," Detective Calloway said as one of the uniformed officers stepped into the room and grabbed Poe's arm.

"Aye, let her go," I told them, sitting up in my bed.

"Ahmeen Shakur, you have the right to remain silent..."

"No...nooooo!" Poe yelled before she swung on the officer, her fist connecting with his face.

"Poe!" I roared. "She's pregnant!"

"...anything you say can and will be used against you in the court of law..."

"Yo, let her go! Get the fuck off her!" I yelled, suddenly finding strength from God only knows to climb out my bed.

I rushed towards the officer that was manhandling Poetic causing a good fifteen extra men to storm the room. Before I knew it, I was swinging at every last pig that came my way. My heart pumped and felt like a horse was galloping inside of my chest. My body heated, and I kept swinging, only my reflexes were slow. I tried once more to get at the nigga that had put his hands on Poe, but when I drew back to hit him, he rushed me, and that was the last thing that was clear to me before I passed out.

4

POETIC

"Poe! Poe!" Mr. Shakur called after me as I ran as fast as I could towards the elevator.

I pressed down on the button hard and fast like my life depended on. I had to get out of here. I had been sitting by Ahmeen's side since the doctors had come and told us that he'd made it through but was in very critical condition. Mr. Shakur and I both had never left, waiting for the moment that he opened his eyes and graced us with the sound of his voice.

They kept telling us that it would be any moment, and although Ahmeen had finally awakened and scared the shit out of me, I was excited to see that he really was okay. Hearing the doctors tell me that he was going to make it was a relief, but seeing it with my own eyes had been exactly what I needed to finally breathe. Sad to say that it ended up with Ahmeen being arrested for Quavo's death where he would be hauled off to jail the moment he was well enough.

Seemed like life wouldn't slow down for me. Ever since Melody's death, it'd been like a whirlwind of chaos. I didn't know how much more of it I could take. With a new baby coming, I needed peace and stability, but my life was everything but that. Either way, just like

Ahmeen had just went hard for me in that room, I was going to do the same for him.

"Poe!" Mr. Shakur called out to me again just as the elevator dinged and opened.

I stepped on the inside and quickly pressed the number one button. I didn't feel like talking to anyone but the person that I was leaving here to see, which was Herbo. I needed him to clear up a lot of shit for me right now, starting with all of this mess that Lyric had started, which I knew was the reason the police was after Ahmeen for Quavo's murder.

I couldn't believe how jealous of a bitch my own sister was of me. She had gone too damn far and seeing how everyone had taken her side and immediately believed her was enough to keep my distance. I was no longer hurt that they thought that I was capable of hurting Melody, but more so angry that they were that damn gullible. Any smart person could see that Lyric was lying through her damn teeth. I had seen her murder Steve in cold blood, and it was obvious that that wasn't the first time she had killed someone.

"Poetic!"

The elevator doors stopped and reopened only seconds before they were about to close. I bit down on the inside of my cheeks as I gripped at my side. Twinges of pain nagged at me, and I did my best to ignore it, hoping that everything was fine with me and my baby. I knew stress could cause me to miscarry, but it wasn't like I could do anything to stop the world from crumbling down around me.

"I gotta go," I told him, dismissively, hoping he would take that and just leave me alone.

"You need to go home. You're pregnant and haven't rested or barely eaten in three days," he said and I shrugged.

"I'll rest and eat when I know that Ahmeen is okay."

"Ahmeen will be fine. I have some of the best lawyers in the country headed down here, and he will be out of custody in a matter of hours. When he is released, he will want to know that you're okay."

"I'm fine, but I have something that I need to do. Just tell Ahmeen to call me, and I will come back up here."

"And where are you going?" he asked me, and I looked up at him and frowned.

"I just said that I have something to do."

"And I just asked you where are you going?"

I sucked my teeth and rolled my eyes, before I leaned against the back of the elevator. I wasn't about to answer him. It was crazy because him and Ahmeen acted just alike. Bossy and as cocky as ever, but if he thought that it moved me, then he had truly lost his shit. I crossed my arms over my chest and clicked my tongue, prepared to have a stare down with him until he allowed the elevator to close and me to be on my merry way.

"Stubborn, I see. Go on. I'll see you when you get back," Mr. Shakur told me, and I quickly pressed the number one again and the button that shut the doors.

Mr. Shakur grimaced at me, and I annoyedly rolled my eyes before becoming antsy from the elevator taking so long to reach my floor. Finally when it did, I stormed off while pulling my cell phone from my purse. I scrolled through my contacts until I made it to Herbo's name and then pressed down on it.

The line trilled once I placed it to my ear, and once I picked my head up and stepped on the outside of the elevator, two of Ahmeen's detail was standing in front of me. I frowned and tried to walk around them, but they only moved back in my way, not allowing me to leave. My palms became sweaty, as I dropped the phone by my side, and I glared over at my shoulder at Mr. Shakur who stood near the sliding doors of the hospital.

"We got her," the biggest one, whom I knew as Latrel said.

"Got me for what?" I questioned, my head cocking to the side.

"We'll take you wherever you need to go, but we've been ordered to first take you home so that you can shower, eat, and then sleep for a few hours," Latrell told me, and I took a couple of steps back.

"No!" I yelled.

"It's up to you, Ms. King. You either allow us to take you home, or you go back inside with Mr. Shakur."

"Y'all got me fucked up. I'mma grown ass woman. I drove my own car here, and I can drive my shit to where I need to go, now excuse me," I urged, and tried to move around them, but both of their big asses surrounded me.

"Hello...Poe!" I heard, remembering that I had called Herbo.

"Oh sorry," I told him as I quickly brought the phone back to my ear. "I need to see you, but later. Can you meet me somewhere?"

"Yea, of course, is everything okay?" he asked me, and I shook my head as if he could see me.

"No...and I need you to help me so bad, but I can't talk right now. Please just be by your phone in a few hours, and I will call you back," I told him and hung up.

Frustrated tears leaked from my eyes. All I wanted to do was get everything cleared up so that when Ahmeen recovered, he could come home where he belonged. I knew that Mr. Shakur was doing what he thought was best for me, but I was so aggravated that he was stepping in at the wrong time. I needed to handle this on my own. I felt like it was the only thing that would make me feel better and knowing that I had to wait made me so mad.

I broke down crying like a baby as defeat took over. With pouty lips, I crossed my arms over my chest and allowed the security to take me to their car. I guess a shower and a couple of hours of sleep would be okay, but I knew I wasn't going to eat shit. I was too sick to my stomach to eat anything. I was too stressed and too worried, so I wasn't even going to try.

Hours later, and I had to admit that my body felt a lot better. I had gone home, took a nice long bath, and slept for over four hours. I also packed me and Ahmeen a bag of clothes and snacks, because I wasn't leaving the hospital until he was walking out with me. When I had gotten everything that I needed, I had Latrel take me back to the hospital and had texted Herbo to meet me there in the waiting area.

It was a little after eight at night as we rode through the streets of Atlanta that were wet from the rain that had fallen earlier in the day.

The air was becoming cool, and I couldn't help the memories of days when Ahmeen and I would lay up and watch Netflix on days like this. We would always start something new, end up kissing, then fucking, and then sleeping all before the movie was even over. The thought of it caused me to chuckle and rub my stomach knowing that it was the exact reason I was in the position that I was in now.

"You alright back there?" Latrel asked as he veered at me through the mirror.

"Yea, I'm good…" I told him, as I pulled up the last message I had gotten from Ahmeen the day everything had gone down.

Ahmeen: *You got your necklace back yet? Hurry up and get back man. Crazy how much I been missing your ass when we're apart. I can't stand it bae and so glad that we making this next step to move in together.*

I shook my head and smiled as I read over the message. It was like I had lost my family, but I gained the love of my life at the same time. I never wanted to pick one over the other, but I knew that my heart wouldn't lead me wrong. I loved Ahmeen so much and although things were rough right now, I couldn't wait until we got back to our Netflix and Chill days with our bad ass baby in the middle of us.

"We here, little mama. Let's go," Latrel informed me, and I glared out of the window at the hospital, noticing the heavy police presence. Latrel grabbed my bags from me, and followed behind me as I went inside. "Thank you."

"Of course," he replied.

The waiting area was packed, but I was able to find some empty chairs in the corner of the room. Soon as Latrel sat my bags down, I looked down at the time on my phone and then took a seat while I waited for Herbo to show. It seemed like the time slowly ticked away as I checked the clock damn near every few minutes. I was starting to feel like Herbo wasn't going to show, and when I went to send him a text message, my phone lit up with his name on the screen.

"Hello," I said into the receiver of my phone.

"What's up? Where you at?" Herbo asked me, and I sat forward in my seat and looked around.

When I spotted Herbo coming through the front, I stood up and waved him over to where I was. His tall stature commanded the attention of every woman in the room. Even in the state that he was in, he looked well put together and not like he had been through hell and back just as I had. The closer he got to me, the cologne he was wearing tickled my nostrils and it immediately made me think of Maino. Them niggas acted more like twins than Lyric and I did, and they weren't even related for real. They enjoyed the same things, would cop some of the same outfits and shoes, and loved them some Sean John cologne. I couldn't believe that their friendship was now just a distant memory. I never once thought that it would be like this, but I also never thought I would no longer have my brother in my life either.

"He's good," I told Latrel when he had quickly stepped in front of Herbo.

I smirked a little when Herbo mugged Latrel and then walked around him to get to me. I hugged him, his tall frame towering over me as he held onto me for a long while. I could feel how tense he was and knew that he was carrying the weight of the world on his back. He took a seat, and I sat back down in the chair that I had been sitting in before he arrived.

It was like I could sense eyes on me, and when I looked to my left, I could see Mr. Shakur staring directly at us. I gave him a sympathetic smile, before I rolled my eyes and sucked my teeth. The way he was hovering over me was weird, but then again, this was how my father was with me as well.

"Lyric...I heard Steve telling her the other night that you were coming at him for information about the night Melody was killed."

"Yea...after you told me who he was, I went and found where he be at. But I hadn't been able to catch up to him yet," Herbo said and I shook my head.

"Lyric killed him. Did you know that?"

"What?" he exclaimed, clearly shocked by my admission.

"She stabbed him like it wasn't nothing." I said and winced as images of Lyric shoving the knife into the side of Steve's neck popped into my head. "I heard him telling her that she needed to give him more money or else she was going to let you know that he was hired by her to kill me and Loop. And how Melody was just an innocent casualty."

"Yoooo, I can't believe this shit. Are you fucking serious?"

"That's not the end of it. Lyric somehow made it to my parents before I did. She was able to make them believe that I did all of it, and because I am dealing with Ahmeen, everyone believed her. I didn't do any of that shit, Herbo, and you gotta tell them that. I don't care about them being mad at me for who I chose to fall in love and have a baby with, but I refuse to allow my name to be tarnished for something I didn't do. I love my sister Melody, and I would never..." my voice cracked, as tears skipped down my face.

"Aye, shit. This is a lot. You fuckin' with Ahmeen?" he asked and looked over at Mr. Shakur. "That's why that nigga over there. Yo, who in the hospital right now?"

"Someone shot Ahmeen...I don't know. We don't know anything yet," I lied, knowing I couldn't tell him that Moni was responsible. My thoughts were suddenly lost as I looked over at Mr. Shakur who was coming closer to us. "But, I need you to tell them that, Herbo. Please? I didn't do anything. Oh...another thing. Lyric told everyone that I sent Dez a message on Instagram telling him that Quavo was the one to kill Mrs. Shakur. I never told anyone that, and I damn sure didn't send no message. She's saying that I got him killed, but how would she know that, Herbo, if she's not the one that did it? Not to mention, the police came up in here earlier today saying that Ahmeen killed Quavo. They've arrested him for his murder, but he didn't do this. I know he didn't. It had to be Lyric. She seemed too comfortable with the way that she killed Steve like she had done it plenty of times before. You gotta help me clear our names, Herbo. You the only person that seems to know besides me that Lyric is full of shit."

Herbo suddenly started shaking. I could see every vessel in his face and neck start to protrude, and I knew at that point that I had said something to tick him off. I wasn't trying to upset him, but I wanted him to help me. He was my only resource at this point. Lyric had taken down innocent men, and now she was trying to take me and Ahmeen down too. She had to be stopped and since everyone seemed to think that she was a victim, I knew I was going to need help to prove what she was hiding.

"Yo, if this shit is true, I'm killing that hoe. Just know that," Herbo promised as he sniffled and quickly swiped at his face. "I never met a muthafucka as evil as that bitch. Can't believe I crossed my mans for her."

"She tricked all of us...don't be mad at yourself," I told him, and he rushed to his feet.

"Yo, take care of yourself. I'll hit Maino up and see what I can do, but the nigga been put me on the block list after everything went down with me and Lyric. I'll be in contact, though," Herbo told me before he walked off.

"Everything okay over..." Mr. Shakur started, and I stood up from my chair and stared at him while cutting him off.

"Yea, daddy, what did they say about my baby daddy?" I sarcastically asked causing him to smirk.

"He'll be arraigned in the morning. They'll have a judge come down and take care of it here. The lawyers are sure that he will get bail and of course I'll post it as soon as he does. For now, we're having a bed delivered to y'alls house and his boy Turner and the doctor... um, Doctor Obudawala will take turns taking care of him at the house along with a team of nurses."

"Good," I smiled.

"So, we wait."

"I guess that's all we can do. Maybe this is a good time to get to know my daughter. Have a seat."

5

LYRIC

I was sitting inside of my bedroom, back at my parents' house while scrolling through my Instagram feed. I was bored out of my mind, but with everything that had been going on, nobody would let me leave the house. They feared that I was going to go run to Herbo or that Poe was going to do something or have something to done to me. Imagine that? Me being scared of Poe when I knew she wasn't capable of harming a fly. She was just that dumb and that naïve that setting her up for everything that I had done, didn't take much effort at all. Especially being that she was fucking with the enemy. She had dug her own damn grave and although I had planned something much worse for her and Ahmeen, the events that had led up to this had made more sense.

Mama: *Come here to the family room. I need to talk to you.*

I looked at the notification that popped up at the top of my phone and then rolled my eyes. Getting out of bed, I slid my PINK flip flops on and walked out of my room and down the stairs. Crossing my arms over my chest, I made my way to the family room where I found my mama, daddy, and Maino all sitting on the sofa with stoic looks on their faces.

"Yes?" I asked, looking at each of them.

"Lyric...tell us again what happened at the apartment," my mama started, and I frowned.

"What you mean?" I probed, my palms becoming sweaty as I noticed the way Maino was looking at me.

"Tell us what happened the night at your apartment...you know when Steve was killed...by Poe...right?" my mother quizzed, and I sighed, annoyedly.

"I told you what happened. I don't wanna keep talking about it. I'm really..."

"Girl, tell me what the fuck happened and now!" she yelled, causing every inch of my body to tremble. "Cause I'm confused as fuck right now and I wanna make sure I got my shit all the way together before I go upside your damn head."

"I told you what happened! Steve got mad and started demanding money from me...I mean from Poe. He was tryna make her pay more for killing Melody."

"Nah, you said that shit right the first time. He was demanding money from your ass and you killed him. Herbo came to see me a couple of hours ago. I wasn't even gonna let him in, but something told me I should. He told me that Poe called him up and gave her side of the story. He also told me that he did some research and found out that Steve was there the night that Melody was killed. He even has pictures of him being here," Maino's ugly ass said, and I sniffled and shook my head. He thought he was so smart.

"Not only that, Poe told him that she walked up on you and Steve's conversation and the nigga was telling you that he wanted more money from you and how if you didn't give it to him, he was gonna let Herbo know that you wanted Poe and Loop killed and that Melody was just in the wrong damn place at the wrong damn time."

"That's not true!" I screamed, tears pinching the corners of my eyes. *Fuck Herbo's little dick ass,* I thought to myself as I stepped back a couple of feet.

"Yea, I didn't wanna think it was true myself until the police informed us that they finally finished combing through the footage of the college's surveillance cameras. Poe never came inside. She stood by the door and then after a few minutes, she took off running. So how the hell did she kill Steve if she never came inside?" Maino stood to his feet and came at me.

"Why would you do something like this? Do you know how bad Melody's death has crushed this entire family? And not only that, we done pushed Poe into the hands of them niggas on some lies you fed us?" my father interjected, and I shook my head relentlessly.

"It's not true. Poe did do it. I didn't do any of that. She murdered Steve! She had Melody killed, not me!"

"Stop lying little girl. I told you that little heifer needed help a long damn time ago. I should've known her ass was sitting here putting on a damn show the whole time," my mama stated, and I frowned at her as tears slid down my face. "Poe's ass wrong as hell for talking to that Shakur boy, but I should've known my baby wouldn't do this. She loved Melody."

"Your baby?" I chuckled to keep from crying.

"I don't know, Lyric. This shit is so farfetched that I don't even know what to do with you. You got your own sister killed and then set the other one up..."

"But I didn't..." I interjected, placing my hand over my chest. "I loved Melody, too. Can I please just grab me a drink of water? I can't breathe...Oh, my, God. My chest feels like it's tightening...."

"Yea, I bet it is. Go on and bring your ass right back. I think I know what I'm going to do with you. Y'all think that y'all are going to keep doing dumb shit and that daddy is just going to bail you out each time, but not this time. This shit is sickening," my daddy stated, and I swallowed back as fear replaced every feeling that I currently felt.

I quickly exited the family room and thought about running out the front door but when I saw that Maino was staring right at me, I knew it wasn't possible. I knew that if I tried to run, I wouldn't even get far.

A couple of days ago, I had overheard them speaking and knew that Maino had done something that had everyone on high alert. They had doubled security over the last few days because of it, and anything leaving or coming without approval was like signing your own death warrant. The way they were treating me, I knew I wouldn't make it out of here alive. They never liked me. It was so evident in the way that they treated me. I was the black sheep of this family even though I tried so hard to be liked by everyone. They didn't love me, so they wouldn't mind me leaving.

I swallowed back the lump that formed in my throat and slowly walked into the huge, open kitchen. Each step felt like I was walking through drying cement as I made my way over to the refrigerator. All my shit had caught up to me, and I didn't even know what else they had known that I had done. Did they know that I was the one that had inboxed Dez and told them about Quavo killing LaShonda even though I knew that it was actually Maino. I wondered if they knew that I had actually tried to kill Poe almost every year since the moment I realized I hated her. She had always been on my hit list, however the bitch always made it through. I had done a lot of bad stuff over the years, a lot.

"Hurry the hell up, Lyric!" I heard my mama yell.

I sucked my teeth and then pulled the refrigerator open to grab a bottle of cold water. Twisting the top off, I took a few sips while staring at the countertop that was directly across from me. It was like my soul was drawn to the shininess that poked out from the bamboo holder that sat there. I walked over to it and replaced the water bottle with the shiny knife that stuck out. It was huge, almost as big as the kind that you would see in a butcher shop. I saw the chef that would come to our house sporadically use it cut through the bones of meat, so I knew how sharp it was.

"Lyric..." my mama's voice echoed and with how clear it sounded just then, I knew that she was close to me.

Looking at the ridges of the knife, I bit down on my bottom lip and seemed to dig my feet into the floor beneath me. I didn't even think any further and just went from one side of my neck to the other.

It wasn't even painful where I had cut myself. The thing that hurt the most was the throb that suddenly ripped through my chest like a hot fire. I couldn't breathe. I couldn't speak.

"Aghhhhhhhhhhhhhh!" I heard my mother scream.

I turned to face her, her eyes wide as her hands covered her mouth. She looked more scared than she did hurt. I didn't see the first tear fall from her eyes, though, and that bothered me, and made me not regret anything that I ever done. I would rather be dead than to live with knowing that once again, Poe had gotten one up on me.

Fuck it, I thought before I fell face first into the floor.

6

AHMEEN

6 Months Later…

"Your honor, we must tell you that Mr. Shakur is Atlanta's problem. He has fed our city with the deadly heroin that has been the cause of many of our doctors, nurses, lawyers, teachers and not to mention kids being hooked or either found dead in their homes," the DA said, and I sighed and pulled at my tie.

"Objection, Your Honor! I ask that the false statement and ludicrous accusations be strickened from the record. We are here because my client, Mr. Shakur is being accused of murder. These accusations of being a drug dealer are far-fetched, and an attempt to taint my client's image with the jury because the DA realizes that they have no case," my attorney, Donovan Marshall, argued.

I sat back in my seat and clasped my hands calmly underneath my chin. Six whole months later, and I was in perfect health, richer than I had ever been and more feared than I ever thought possible. The dope game was mine and I had built an empire so large that even these fucked up ass murder charges wouldn't change that. One monkey didn't stop no show, and while Moni had tried to take me out, he had only made a nigga want it more than ever.

Since the bitch was hiding out in protective custody and I couldn't get at him like I wanted, it was only right that I stunted on his ass. I was pretty sure that wherever he was, living his fucked up, snitching ass life, he heard about all the strides that I was making, and I knew it had him sick. I was living it up, and once I beat these murder charges, he was going to either have to put a bullet in his own head or step out, so I could handle it for him.

"Sustained..." the judge concurred. "Stick to the facts of the case please DA Lewis."

I veered over my shoulder and one by one made eye contact with everyone that was sitting on the front row behind me. My pops, Goat and Jyelle, and Poetic was holding onto our newborn son Ahmeen. I bit my lip as my eyes lingered over my baby, wondering if four weeks was too soon for me to slide up in her. She'd given birth to the lil' one a little early, but just like his pops, my youngin' was a fighter and came out weighing six pounds even, with his thumb in his mouth.

I had to give it up to my legal team. They had come through and had gotten me off on bail and had done everything they could to postpone this trial. Because of them, I hadn't missed a step when it came to Poe and our kid, or the drug game. Whenever I wasn't in the streets, I spent that time with my family. Me and Poe's bond was closer than ever, and I swear being with her was the best decision I ever made. She made a nigga feel high, no dope. I wished that I could give her everything, but money couldn't buy what she truly wanted which was for her family to accept that she had chosen to be with me.

"Your Honor, in reference to the case against my client..."

"Bro, you told Kiani to come?" Goat whispered into my ear as he tugged at my shoulder.

I frowned and slightly turned my body just as Kiani took a seat next to her father Quentin. She held onto her baby tightly as she gave me a smile that I returned with a mug. I guess Poe caught on and twisted into her seat so that she could follow my line of vision.

"Bruh, get her the fuck up outta here!" I whispered harshly before turning back to face the court.

"You want me to tell her to leave?" Goat asked me and I glared at him, wondering if he had lost his shit.

"Yea...nigga!" I said a little too loud.

Everyone in the courtroom looked at me and my lawyer gave me a quick tap to let me know to pipe it down. My leg bounced up and down as nervousness began to set in. I didn't even give a fuck about what was going on in front of me now. Kiani being here was a big fucking problem.

For the past six months I had managed to keep her away from Poe and vice versa. She'd had the baby a few months ago and I stepped up to be a father, but I wasn't telling that to Poe. Every time I thought about it, I knew what it would do to her, so I didn't say shit. She had been through enough as it was, and I wasn't trying to add more problems to my baby's life. When she saw me, she smiled big and that shit lit up my life. When she cried, it messed with me bad and I did whatever I could to try to fix it. But Kiani having my first kid wasn't something that I could correct.

"The trial will proceed, prosecution call your first witness," the judge ordered, and the commotion behind us got everyone's attention.

"Why the fuck do I gotta leave? No, me and my son have a right to be here like everyone else!" Kiani screamed, her voice shaky.

"Kiani..." Quentin said to her, and I glared over my shoulder at them.

"No fuck that! You can kiss their ass if you want, but I'm not going to! Keep playing with me, Ahmeen!"

I shook my head, took in a deep breath and let it all out again. Turning back around, the judge was burning a hole through my face as he stared at me unfavorably. I couldn't wait to leave here so I could get all in her shit. I had told her that I didn't want her or the baby here when she asked if it was okay to come and show her support. I made sure to let Quentin know my wishes as well. My life was on the line and here Kiani's ass was acting like a damn fool, giving these muthafuckas a reason to look at me even crazier than they already were.

"If we can get a little order here then we can proceed. Are you ready to start, Mr. Shakur?" The judge said snobbishly, and I sucked my teeth and nodded my head. "Very well, if the prosecution can call their first witness please?"

"Your Honor, we would like to call De'Moni Shakur to the stand," the prosecution said, and I glared back at my pops and Goat before turning back towards the front.

After a couple of minutes, De'Moni's bitch ass walked in and took his rat ass over to where the ballot swore him in. He got on the stand and then placed his eyes on me. I wanted to salute the nigga to let him know he had showed the fuck out. He really had, not only turned fed, but had tried to kill a nigga too. He'd gone as far as to telling them about me killing that nigga Quavo. The bitch was really tryna take me down.

"Mr. De'Moni Shakur, on or about the day of August 10th, 2017, what were you doing?" the DA Lewis asked Moni.

"I was out with my girlfriend, I believe we saw a movie and went to dinner that day," he lied.

"And after the movie, what happened?"

"I was called to come to a warehouse that my father owns."

"What type of business is done out of that warehouse?"

"It's a trucking company. My father does shipments for some of the major distributors like Amazon, Walmart and places like that," Moni said, sounding like a preppy ass white boy.

"Would you say that drugs are moved from that warehouse?" the DA asked causing my lawyer to jump to his feet.

"Objection! Relevancy Your Honor." My lawyer yelled

"What exactly are you getting at, DA Lewis?" the judge asked him, and he crossed his arms over his chest.

"You're Honor, we're trying to prove that the defendant is a murderous drug lord that, not only pumps fear into the streets, but a deadly drug as well," the DA told him, and I grimaced.

"We're here because my client is being accused of murder, not being this drug lord that you accuse him of. The witness is actually here testifying against my client because he got caught with a large sum of drugs, and even caught distributing to a very known drug kingpin that has been on the FBI's radar for years," Marshall argued, and I sat back in my seat and clasped my hands together.

"Your Honor, the witness is not on trial here!" DA Lewis yelled.

"Well, he should be. How can we trust what he is saying here today when he's trying to get his way out of a life sentence," Marshall said with a shrug.

"Your Honor..."

"Stop it! Stop it right now! DA Lewis, please keep the line of questions about what you are trying to prove here and the jury will disregard Attorney Marshall's statement. Now, if you two cannot act civilized, we will have to reconvene."

"No problems here," DA Lewis said and my attorney only shrugged. "Now...Moni, let's get back to the day in August that you went to the warehouse. What was the reason that you were called there?"

"My brother had called me. Told me that he'd found out who murdered our mother and that he had the person there at the warehouse," Moni continued his lies.

"And your brother...you have two right?"

"Yes, I have two younger brothers. Ge'Loni and Ahmeen."

"And which brother is it that called you."

"Ahmeen."

"And is Ahmeen here today?"

"Yes, he is."

"Can you point him out for me?" the DA asked him, and Moni pointed at me. "Let the record reflect that the witness has pointed out the defendant, Ahmeen Shakur."

"Noted..." the judge stated.

"So, tell us what happened once you arrived at the warehouse, Mr. Shakur?"

"Soon as I walked in, Ahmeen was standing there, the guy, Quavarious was bloody. He had been beaten to the point that you could barely recognize him. I asked Ahmeen what was going on and he'd told me that he'd found the guy and before I could even ask him was he sure about it, he shot him in the forehead."

"When you say him? You mean Quavarious, correct. Ahmeen shot Quavarious in the head?"

"Yes, Ahmeen, my little brother shot Quavarious in the head."

Everyone in the room started to gasp as I anxiously tapped my fingers against the table. I couldn't even take my eyes off of Moni as he sat there with a smug look on his face. The amount of betrayal and deceit was immeasurable. The nigga was on one and I still couldn't figure out what I had done to him to make him hate me this much.

I tugged at my tie and cleared my throat before sitting back in my seat and sighing. Yea, I had shot Quavo, but Moni was the one that had beat him senseless. Shit the nigga was already half-dead before I arrived, and I had only finished him off. I knew he wasn't that mad because I was the one to pull the trigger and not him. Even then, I should've known better than to get my hands dirty in front of anyone.

"Bruh..." Goat tapped me again on my shoulder, and I turned slightly to see what he'd wanted.

"Poe ran out. You want me to go after her?" he asked me, and I quickly scanned the room.

"If she don't come back in five minutes, yea," I told him and he nodded.

"So, Mr. Shakur, why didn't you tell anyone what happened that day? Are you aware that not reporting a crime...especially one such as murder is considered a crime as well?" DA Lewis asked, and Moni nodded.

"Yes, I'm aware, however Ahmeen threatened to kill me and my girlfriend if I told anyone. I was scared of what he might do to me."

"Bitch ass nigga..." I grimaced, causing the entire courtroom to erupt, some in my favor and some not.

Soon as I walked up out of here today, Moni was a dead man. Fuck it.

7

POETIC

"It's ok baby. Mommy is about to feed you right now," I cooed onto Little Ahmeen's ear as I stepped out of the restroom.

Hearing Moni sit there and testify on his own brother was sickening. I couldn't even bear to sit and listen to it any longer and had just stormed out of the courtroom before I said something that would get Ahmeen in trouble. These past six months of my life had been like a roller coaster of emotions. A bitch had to pray to God that when a good day came that it would last forever.

One thing I could say was that Ahmeen did everything in his power to make me happy. Even though he was facing his own shit he'd always put me first. After he'd gotten shot, I had tried everything to nurse him back to health but he was persistent that I relaxed and allowed him to handle himself. He was so strong never really showing that anything affected him unlike myself.

Most days, I could barely keep together. I missed my parents and my brothers. I wanted so bad for things to get back to the way they once were but situations that had occurred had made it impossible for that to happen. One thing that was for certain was that I wasn't leaving my man. I loved him and this kid that was his freaking twin to death. My family didn't accept him, especially since he was sitting on trial for Quavo's murder.

Ahmeen was guilty for sure. He had done everything but deny that he had killed Quavo to me. I asked and he never said yes, but definitely never said no to me. I was so mad and hurt about it because Quavo was like family to me, but I had to remember that Meen was out for revenge for his mama. Even if the senseless tip they had received from Lyric was false, they hadn't just killed Quavo for nothing. I was glad her flaw ass hadn't given up her brother like she had given me up.

Speaking of Lyric's mentally insane ass, I hadn't spoken to anyone but Chuck in my family to know that she was still in a mental asylum. I never asked about her or entertained any thoughts of conversation that concerned Lyric. She was as good as dead to me. Because of her, I had lost my family. They didn't trust me and I didn't trust them so we all just kept our distance.

"Excuse me, Poetic right?" I heard someone ask just as I was heading back into the dreadful courtroom.

"Yea..." I turned around to see Kiani standing there with a baby in her hands. I stared at him for a long while, as he dribbled from the sides of his mouth. He was chocolate like Ahmeen, with fat and chubby cheeks. "...Kiani, right?"

"Yes girl. I mean last time we saw each other turned out to be really tragic so we didn't get a chance to get formally acquainted, but yes I'm Kiani. It's not to formally meet you. You know since it seems that Meen doesn't want us to ever see each other," Kiani said before I finally looked her in the face.

"What you mean?" I asked her, switching little Ahmeen from one side to the other. He was barely a month old and already heavy as hell. "Why wouldn't he want us seeing each other? But why do we need to?"

"I've asked him several times to let me meet you, you know you have a newborn too and I'm sure like me you wouldn't want your baby around other women unless you got a chance to know them. Not saying that you're a bad person, but you know just want to know who's going to be around Little Ahmeen, you know?" Kiani said and I frowned.

"Little Ahmeen?" I questioned, my heart suddenly pounding like crazy.

"Yes, his name is Ahmeen Shakur, Jr and he 8 months old. I would ask if you would like to hold him, but you already got your hands full," she laughed and it felt like I was about to pass out.

"So, this is supposed to be Ahmeen's baby and his name is Ahmeen...too?" I asked her just to be sure this bitch wasn't fucking with me.

"...yes, as many times he's been to your house girl, you telling me you didn't know his name?" Kiani asked as she looked at me strangely. "And it's crazy cause he never mentioned to me that you were pregnant or even had a child."

"Aye, Poe," I heard from behind me.

I glanced over my shoulder to see Goat coming my way followed by his father, Mr. Shakur. My eyes burned with tears that I did my best to hold back. If the trial hadn't been enough, this broad Kiani had added even more to my plate. For her to be sitting here saying she had a baby with the exact same name as my child and that the baby had been to my house was ludicrous. I had never heard of her baby or her for that matter. Kiani wasn't even a fucking subject between me and Ahmeen. As far as I knew, they were over and hadn't had any communication but I guess it was obvious that sucka ass nigga was lying.

"Kiani, what's up, where's your pops at?" Mr. Shakur asked her, and she slightly smiled.

"He's in the car waiting for me. I just want to say that I don't appreciate not being able to come to court and the way y'all pushing us out. That was really uncalled for and embarrassing," Kiani told him and he shrugged.

"Just giving my son his wishes so that he feels as comfortable as possible through this ordeal," Mr. Shakur told her as my head continued to spin.

"Comfortable? So, me and Meen's child make things less comfortable? Ok, I get it. And is that because Meen seems to have..."

"Poe, let's go..." I heard Meen call out.

I looked up at him, his tall stature towering over me as he walked towards where we all stood. Apparently, court had dismissed for the day. I could tell that he was upset. I mean anybody would be upset if their own flesh and blood sat in a courtroom and ratted them out. I was upset for him, but I was even more upset that the nigga had been lying to me all this time. I couldn't even begin to understand it. I felt like he was living a double life while my dumb ass was thinking I was living a fairytale with him.

"So, me and your son make things uncomfortable for you?" Kiani asked, coming close to Ahmeen.

He suddenly snatched our son from my arms and held onto him like he was a football. He didn't even look at Kiani while I couldn't stop staring at the desperation on her face. The look she wore told me she hadn't just made things all up. She was just as hurt as I was and just as confused.

"Really, so you gonna fucking ignore me. Act like we don't fucking exist cause your little girlfriend is right here!" Kiani screamed, near tears.

"Yo, Poe, I said let's go!" Ahmeen barked and this time I moved.

Ahmeen tried to reach for my hand but I folded my arms across my chest while following behind him. He had me fucked up. I wasn't going to say anything right now, not in front of everyone. I wouldn't give muthafuckas the satisfaction of seeing me sweat, especially not Kiani. But soon as we got home, I was getting all in his shit.

Once we had gotten into the car and headed home, neither of us had said a word to each other. I could tell that Ahmeen was doing his best to feel me out, while I was doing everything I could to keep it together. I had needed to gather my thoughts and ration out if I had wanted to kill him first, or fuck someone else so he could feel exactly how I felt at this moment. My entire body was shaking on the inside and I didn't know who I wanted to be mad at the most. Ahmeen or the people around me that smiled in my face knowing that I was being lied to on a daily basis.

Seeing that little chocolate baby that had my baby's same name had me really heated inside. None of this even made sense to me. Our baby had just been born. Kiani's had been here for months. Why would Ahmeen first allow her to give their baby his name, and then allow me to name him the same thing? It was so fuckin' disrespectful and the more I thought about it, the more my heart felt like it was tearing into pieces.

Ahmeen had been going on and on about his heir and how he was ecstatic to be having his first son and someone to carry on his name and legacy in the future. We had even set him up a trust fund, naming him as Ahmeen's only beneficiary, but what about him and Kiani's son? Mannnn, I was so lost and confused right now.

The moment we pulled up to the house, I was pushing the door open before the truck could even pull up to a complete stop. I practically ran inside and went up the stairs to our bedroom. I stripped out of my clothes and headed straight for the shower. I just wanted to escape and get away from him, but when he stepped into the shower and closed the door behind him, I could only turn around and stare at him.

Ahmeen stood there, looking like he'd just stepped out of GQ magazine. The denim blue looking suit that he wore along with the red tie, would have a naïve person thinking that he was just a businessman that had been caught up in something that wasn't him. I knew better. The more I was around Ahmeen, the more I grew to learn how vicious he was. He had his shit with him, and it was so crazy how much he reminded me of my father and Maino. There streets were them, and without the streets they wouldn't survive.

"You okay?" Ahmeen questioned as he removed his jacket, followed by his tie.

He dropped them both at his feet and started to unbutton the collar shirt that he wore. Numerous tattoos were on display as he continued to remove every piece of clothing that he was wearing. His dark skin was free of any blemishes besides the evidential gunshot wounds that he had suffered months ago. He licked his thick lips as he eyed me sexily and made one step closer to me.

"I asked if you was okay?" Ahmeen repeated and I nodded my head, before my hands suddenly covered my body.

I wasn't fat and had only weighed about ten pounds more than I had before giving birth, but my stomach wasn't as flat as it used to be. My boobs were big as hell now, and they didn't quite sit up like they used to. Ahmeen had never made a complaint, but truthfully, I had never really allowed him to see me fully naked since I had given birth. I was insecure, and him staring at me like he wanted me was only making that feeling worse.

"Stop looking at me," I told him before I turned and walked towards the glass, shower doors. I opened them and turned the knob towards the H.

"A.J. is in his bassinet, sleeping. I'm gonna go downstairs and workout with the trainer. Be back up in about an hour. Was thinking I could get the chef over to cook us up something," Ahmeen stated and I shrugged.

"Yea..." was all I said before I got into the shower.

Ahmeen stood near the doorway, and I could feel his eyes on me for a long while before he finally left. When he did, I took in a deep breath, before I suddenly let out everything that I had been holding onto. Tears fell from my eyes, mixing with the water as they hit the base of the floor and washed away through the drain. My heart felt so heavy as it seemed like every single emotion that one could feel took its course through my body.

I washed up and tried to get myself together, but I just couldn't. The more I thought about how treacherous Ahmeen had been, the angrier I became. I hurried out of the bathroom and quickly dressed into a t-shirt and sweats.

After making sure that Little Ahmeen was sleeping, I practically ran out of our bedroom and then quickly descended down the steps. Taking huge strides down the hall until I reached the bottom level door, I pulled it open and went down those stairs, immediately hearing the sound of the treadmill whirring and Ahmeen's feet every time he hit the belt.

Ever since he'd been shot, he'd been working with a trainer at least three days out of the week. He was determined to get his health together, and I commended him for that, because he was way stronger, faster, and healthier than ever.

Once I rounded the corner, my eyes landed on Ahmeen's back while his trainer stood directly next to him. He was running at full speed, faster than I had ever seen, and I wanted to be proud of him, but my anger took over. I rushed towards him and pushed his ass so hard he lost his footing and fell onto the belt hard as hell. I flinched, my eyes narrowing as I watched him bump his head and face before the trainer pulled the emergency plug.

"The fuck!" Ahmeen yelled while looking up at him.

I grimaced before I ran towards him and tried to kick his ass, but his trainer hopped in my way and stopped me. He picked me up from the floor and I wailed in his arms.

"Put me down! Put me down! I'm gonna kill him!" I screamed.

"Aye, put her the fuck down! You lost your fuckin mind nigga?" Ahmeen roared once he finally climbed to his feet.

"Sorry man," the trainer told him.

He moved towards me and the trainer just as I was placed onto the floor. I drew my arms back and tried to slap him when he grabbed it mid-air. The grip he held around my wrist caused tears to sting my eyes. I waited until after the trainer left before I went in on his ass.

"You a fuckin' liar and I'm done with your trifling ass," I said through gritted teeth before my lips started to tremble. I just couldn't hold it in any longer. I finally had to let him know how I felt. "You really was out here hiding a baby nigga?"

He stared at me. The same way he had done when I asked him about Quavo. There was no yes or no. There wasn't even an ounce of him that looked innocent. He only grimaced, looking as if I was wrong for questioning him. His nonchalance and cockiness caused every bit of my soul to pour out that hadn't already moments earlier. I felt weak. Sick to my stomach. Like I was going to die when I realized that it was all real. I didn't understand. I slept with Ahmeen almost every night, spent majority of the day with him besides when he had to meet with his father and brother to handle business.

I guess that was when those visits took place that Kiani was talking about, I thought to myself as I fought to get away from him.

"You really would do this to me? After everything I sacrificed and gave up to be with you," I cried, my heart breaking piece by piece as the seconds went by.

"I was going to tell you. I just didn't wanna stress you out while you was carrying our son," Ahmeen had the nerve to say and I cocked my head to side and looked at him like he was crazy.

"You was going to tell me when? When Ahmeen? Because our son is here now? How long were you going to pretend like he was your first? Your heir, your legacy? All this shit with us is fake right?"

"Ain't shit about us fake, baby. I swear to God. I love the fuck outta you and you know that."

"How the fuck do I know that when you hid a whole fucking baby from me and then lied to my face every damn day! You don't love me nigga." I pushed Ahmeen away and turned to leave.

I wasn't staying here with him. I didn't know where I was going to go, but I couldn't stay another minute in this house. I suddenly felt like the walls were crashing down around me. I don't know what I expected Ahmeen to say, but I damn sure didn't think he would admit that he really did have a child with Kiani. I wanted her to be crazy. I wanted him to tell me that she was a lying bitch and that she was planting a baby on him because she didn't want to let him go, but nope. He really had a kid with her. His first kid!

I knew that it was before me, but that didn't mean that it still didn't hurt. I was crushed. My soul ached, and all I wanted was to call Maino and beg him to come to me. He was the only person that I would ever crawl to when I was hurting. He knew what to say to me and how to make me feel better. That was why I had called him when I had first found out that I was pregnant. Mad or not, him being there for me was everything to me. Man, I missed him so much. I missed my family. Part of me wanted to go home, but the other part feared that I would be judged and ultimately regret running to them.

"Hol' the fuck up! I know you hear me talking to you," Ahmeen yelled after me as I climbed the stairs.

"I don't have anything to say to you. You ain't got shit I wanna hear either. I heard enough. I see what it is."

"Mannnn," he drawled. "I'm sorry, Poe. Shit."

"You sorry? If I had come to you with some shit like this, you would try to break my neck. What if I told you that Ahmeen belonged to Chris and not you." I told him, while looking over my shoulder at him. I could see his jaws flinch and the veins in his neck protruding. "Yea, like I thought."

"That would mean that you really did sleep with that nigga and if that's the case, then I swear to God, I'mma murk the both of y'all."

"Tuh," I waved him off and pushed through the door.

"Bring your ass the fuck here!" Ahmeen ordered and I shook my head and kept it moving.

I went up the stairs that led to our bedroom, my eyes landing on the portrait of Melody that hung on the wall. Somberly, I peeled my eyes away and went into the room and over to my side. I had my own walk-in closet that was filled to capacity with clothes and shoes that I probably wouldn't even live long enough to wear. I started grabbing a few things off of hangars that I could take with me until I figured out what I wanted to do.

"So, you just gon' keep on being disrespectful Poetic and act like I ain't fucking talking to you?"

"Imagine being disrespectful to someone that has lied to your face every damn day for shittttt.... about a year now. I know damn well you had to have known that she was pregnant."

"I didn't know if he was mine so I never said anything about her being pregnant. After she had him, I was just trying to wait until after you had our son. I wasn't trying to stress you more than you already were. With me recovering, your family, the trial and shit...damn, I just never got around to it," Ahmeen said and I shook my head and continued grabbing clothes.

He moved over to where I was, snatched everything I had out of my hand and tossed it onto the floor. I pushed him hard in his firm chest, causing my wrist to bend back and hurt.

"Fuck!" I cried and grabbed my wrist.

"See...you need to keep your damn hands to yourself. Let me see."

"Don't touch me."

"Stop being stubborn man and let me see."

Ahmeen gently grabbed my arm and looked at my wrist. He reached out for my other arm and then pulled me out of the closet and over to the huge ass bed. Sitting down, he pulled me between his legs and looked me over to make sure that I was good.

"You straight."

"I didn't need you to tell me that," I fussed and tried to step back."

"I'm sorry. Every day I wanted to tell you, but I ain't wanna see this. I knew that shit was gon' hurt and that's the last thing I wanted to do was cause you pain. I wanna marry you one day, Poe. Kiani don't mean shit to me and the only thing me and her got going is a co-parenting relationship. I promise you that you don't gotta ever worry about me ever doing shit else to hurt you. This was...was some shit that happened before I could even do anything about it and I just ain't know how to tell you," Ahmeen said and I sighed. "Come on man, we been doing too good. I done seen you crying enough, and you know I don't like that shit."

"We said no more secrets."

"I know. I apologize," Ahmeen told me before he pulled me towards him and kissed my lips.

My ass softened like always and when he laid me down on the bed and began to remove my clothes, I didn't even protest. I allowed him to bury his head between my legs and lick between the folds of my kitty.

"Ohhhh shit," I moaned, my eyes rolling behind my head as passion took over me. "Fuckkkk!"

Ahmeen sucked my love button into his mouth and caused it to immediately swell. He then pulled back before flickering his tongue relentlessly over my clit. I gushed onto his lips and when he removed his shirt and went back in, I locked my legs around his head and grinded my hips into him.

"Make me come!" I told him and grabbed his head. "Shit, damn it, Ahmeen. Fuck!"

"You about to come," he asked, when he came up for air.

"Yea...ummhuh!" I told him, and he went back in.

"You taste so damn good."

Ahmeen sucked and licked for what felt like only a few more seconds before I started shaking like a leaf. I screamed out as more of my juices poured out of me and onto his face. I hadn't been touched since before I had our son, and even though I didn't want this nigga touching me, I couldn't deny how good it all felt.

When he stood up and removed his pants, his dick was pointing right at me, and I licked my lips and opened my legs wider. I had thought that sex with us would get boring, but it never was that way. It was like our lovemaking had intensified. The more we explored each other's bodies, the better things with us had gotten. Ahmeen knew just what to do to me to make me cream all over him, and I knew just how to have him screaming like a bitch.

"Got damn, your shit is soaking," he said as he slid inside of me with ease. "Fuck, you gon' be pregnant again soon cause I ain't pulling out."

"Nope..." I told him, shaking my head adamantly. I shut my eyes closed and then wrapped my arms around Meen's neck. "Yea...right there."

He rocked in and out of me slowly and passionately. Each time he went in, it felt like he was touching the bottom of my stomach. Spreading my legs further, Ahmeen started going deeper and harder causing me to scream out. I placed my hands on his chest and then grew the courage to open my eyes to look at him. I wanted the pleasure, but I also wanted to be mad and knew that when I laid eyes on him, I would forget about it all. His chocolate skin and piercing brown eyes practically melted my heart away.

"You love me?" he smirked, showing his iced out teeth.

"Yea..." I rolled my eyes and refused to keep looking at him.

"Come for me then. Come right now," Ahmeen ordered, but I refused.

"No."

"What the fuck I just say?"

"No...I'm still mad at you," I told him, and his dick felt like it was suddenly in my throat. "Shitttttt!"

"Now!"

"No!"

"Now!"

"Dammn ittttttt! Okay...alright...yes...I will," I said, trying to find my breath.

"What the fuck I say?"

"Alright. You feel it? Huh?" I screamed as an orgasm so big washed over me. I shut my eyes tightly as I rode the euphoric wave that Ahmeen had given to me. "Mmmmh."

"Open your legs back up, I'm about to come, too," Ahmeen grunted and I pulled back.

"Wait..."

Ahmeen suddenly went crazy inside of me. He pumped faster and harder and I gritted down as I waited for him to come. I felt his hard-on seem to widen as he exploded and let it all come in my canal.

"Fuck," he breathed before he rolled over onto the bed.

Ahmeen pulled me into his arms and spooned me from behind. He kissed all over my face and ear for a good while before I heard him suddenly snoring behind me.

I laid there for a good while allowing my thoughts to run wildly through my head. My emotions were always all over the place and it seemed like all I did was think about any and everything that could go wrong.

I knew that Ahmeen had told me that I had nothing to worry about when it came to Kiani and their baby, but I couldn't help but wonder, if that was the case, then why didn't he just tell me the truth. I was still so hurt, and no amount of apologies and sex could change that. All I could do at this point was just think and cry myself to sleep.

8

GE'LONI "GOAT" SHAKUR

That's a vibe (that's a vibe)
She wanna vibe, yeah (wanna vibe)
That's a vibe (that's a vibe)
Yeah, uh (that's a vibe)
That's a vibe (that's a vibe)

I cruised through the streets while bobbing my head to 2 Chainz's *It's a Vibe* track. It was the middle of the day and I had the top of my Lambo down while the air brushed against my skin. Shit felt good and relaxing and was much needed after all the bullshit that was going on. My little brother's child had us all fucked up and on edge.

When I wasn't handling all the backend drug business, I was trying to get at that nigga Moni. The nigga had must've really gone into some ol' secret CIA shit. No matter where I looked, or which of our connects I had gotten in contact with, I couldn't find him. I was the type of nigga that would haunt you down and take your bitch ass out like yesterday's trash. I was itching to get at Moni too. The shit hurt me like a muh'fucka when I found out what he had done to our young bull, and although to this day, I wanted to believe that Ahmeen was mistaken, I knew I had to face reality.

Moni sat in the courtroom today sanging like a little bitch, just lying and shit and the sight of it was just unbelievable. I didn't even know that man that sat up there on that witness stand today. None of us did, which was why I wasn't gonna feel shit when I murked his ass. Meen wanted to get him, but with everything that was going on, I felt like he needed to stand down and act like a fuckin' scholar. Police was watching him too close. He'd been marked as Atlanta's kingpin and the reason behind a lot of white folks' deaths. He was a wanted man and safest thing for him to do was fallback.

"What's up, CoCo?" I said into the phone after answering my first baby mama's call.

"If you don't come and get this bitch, Ge'Loni, I'mma kill this hoe!" CoCo yelled, and I had to pull the phone away to look and make sure I was talking to who I thought I was. CoCo didn't talk like that, at all. "Do you hear me?"

"Come and get who?" I asked her, my forehead wrinkled as I waited for her to answer.

"Your rat face ass baby mama Jyelle...this bitch out here acting a fucking fool. She done broke the windows out my car, and she keeps kicking at my door talking about I'm sleeping with you. Talking about I'm the reason she lost her damn baby. She got the kids scared as shit and it's either you come and get her now, or I kill the hoe. Point, blank, period!"

"A'ight, CoCo, I'm on my way," I told her before I hung up, and made a U-Turn at the next light.

I ran my hands down my face and sighed while I drove as quickly as I could to my baby mama CoCo's house. The feud between her and my current girlfriend and mother of my kids Jyelle had been damn near a decade long. I didn't have nobody but myself to blame for it, but I had hoped that both of them would one day grow up and stop being so damn childish. There was kids involved on both sides and in the end, they were the ones that was truly affected.

CoCo had been in my life way before Jyelle came into the picture. She and I used to date back in high school, but we broke up after I had cheated on her several times. Years went by before we linked again and eventually had our son Gemini.

For whatever reason, we could never get it together, which was why when I ran into Jyelle it was easy to fall for her ratchet ass. Jy was everything that CoCo wasn't. She was full of life, and willing to ride with a nigga through whatever. She didn't press me about this street shit like CoCo always would, and for whatever reason, me and Jy just clicked on a whole 'nother level. Even then, it didn't change the fact that I had mad love for CoCo and my indecisiveness led me to going back and forth between the two for years. Hearts had been broken, kids had been made, and just some more shit that I could never take back. For that reason, Jyelle and CoCo hated each other with a passion. It wasn't even a surprise to get the call that Jy was at her place tripping.

She had suffered a miscarriage a couple of months ago and still hadn't gotten over it yet. For some reason, she blamed me, saying that I had been cheating on her and stressing her out. The night she lost our daughter was the same night she had dreamed that I had sex with CoCo. I wasn't going to lie and act like I didn't hit CoCo every now and then, but it had been a long ass time since I had.

"Bitch, what you mean what am I still doing here hoe?" Jyelle spat the minute I rolled up to CoCo's house.

I hurried up and hopped out the car and ran over to her. She was so busy acting a damn fool that she didn't even see me when I'd come up. I grabbed her from behind and she tried to swang on me until she realized who I was. Her face let on that she was surprised, and then embarrassed, before angry. She snatched away from me and then rushed at CoCo who had stepped out of from behind the screen door.

"Oh, bitch you wanna call my man on me," Jy seethed and swung at her.

Before I knew it, Jyelle had a handful of CoCo's hair and was punching her in the face. I shot up in their direction, and it took everything in me to peel Jyelle off. She had the strength of a mad woman, and I couldn't be mad at nobody but myself. I had played the two of them against each other time and time again and for that reason alone, they couldn't even be in the same vicinity without some shit popping off.

"Let's go! Let's go!" I yelled at Jyelle while her legs dangled in the air.

"I'm not going nowhere until this hoe admit that she has ruined my family," Jyelle screamed, and I sighed when I noticed the neighbors stepping outside.

CoCo lived in a quiet community where it was mostly upper-aged retired families with money. I knew if Jyelle's ass didn't stop, somebody was gonna call twelve.

"You bitch! I swear to God, you bet not ever bring this trifling ass gutta snipe around me no damn more! I'm killing this bitch!" CoCo screamed like she was deranged as blood leaked from her nose and lip.

I looked CoCo over some more before leaving, her brown skin was suddenly stained with the tears that had fallen from her eyes. I wanted to wipe them away for her but knew that I would never hear the end of it if Jyelle saw me. No matter what, CoCo would always have a special place in my heart. She was the mother of two of my kids and had done a lot for me over the years.

"Jyelle, let's go before I knock the shit outta you!" I yelled, trying my hardest to get her little ass to the car.

"Can't believe after all this time, me and this bitch still fighting. This ain't nobody fault but yours. That hoe treat my kids different and you let her...mannnnn," CoCo drawled as she followed behind us.

"I know," I told her as I glared over my shoulder. CoCo's hazel eyes rolled into the back of her head as I eyed her up and down again. "...I apologize."

CoCo reminded me of the chick that was always hosting them *Love and Hip Reunions* Nina Parker. From head to toe, they were damn near identical, only CoCo had some of the most beautiful eyes I had ever seen and wider hips. Hips that a nigga had to pray to stay from being inside of. I had tried many times over the past few months, but she wasn't going for it. When I had told her that Jy was pregnant again, she cut me off and cut me off for real. She had told me many times before that she wasn't going for my shit again, but each time she always gave in. Not this time. This time I could see that she was finally fed up.

"Look, both of y'all listen the fuck up right now!" I yelled, doing my best to hold onto Jyelle's ass. I had her pinned against the car with my back to her, while looking at CoCo. "I never said this shit with the both of you in front of each other, but I apologize for all the shit I have caused between the two of you. I broke both of y'all at some point, and I'm sorry. A nigga ain't have no right going back and forth between the two of y'all. I would love more than anything for the two of you to get along.

I be wanting the kids to have sleepovers and shit. These kids too damn old for me to be having to sneak them around just so they could see each other. They should know their siblings and that shit ain't gonna happen until y'all act right."

"Nigga please, my kids know their siblings and that's the two of them. Gemini and Giaria ain't got no other damn siblings," CoCo spat harshly, and Jy tried to jump from behind me.

"Bitch, fuck your kids!" Jyelle barked.

"Nah, hoe, fuck your bastard ass kids! At least I know 100% without a doubt that my kids are Goat's. Goat, you need to be asking Jyelle why bitches is out here saying that the last baby she was pregnant with, she aborted, not miscarried because she didn't know who the father was and how you need to get a DNA test on the rest," CoCo revealed, and my heart dropped. "That's why that bitch really over here cutting up. She knows her ex-best friend is going around telling everything and being we be in some of the same circles, I know the real."

"Man, stop playing with me," I told CoCo, my arms crossing over my chest as I eyed her. "What ex-best friend?"

"You really gon' sit here and talk to this hoe about some lies?" Jyelle muffed me, and I quickly turned around and was all in her shit.

"Yea...address your hoe! I'mma go back in the house and take care of OUR kids. Get your bitch away from here, Goat. I promise you if that hoe shows up on my doorstep again, she will regret it," CoCo walked off, and I wanted to chase behind her.

I wanted to press about these DNA accusations she was talking about. She knew I ain't play no shit like that. My kids were my life. Regardless of how many I had, neither of them would never question their daddy and the love I had for them. I made sure I got time in with all of them. I was on the same bullshit that Ahmeen was on, having to take my kids to my pops' house just to keep down the confusion between my baby mamas.

"Get your hoe ass in the car!" I told Jyelle, and she moved quickly seeing that I wasn't playing with her.

She rushed around to the passenger's side and quickly let the door up and fell down into the seat. The moment I was inside, I was smashing on the gas and pulling out of the neighborhood. I pressed the Lambo to top speed as I headed towards where Jyelle and I had a home together in the Collier Hills part of Atlanta.

The tension between Jyelle and I at this moment was thick as hell, especially when I kept eyeing her and seeing how she nervously fidgeted with her hands. Looking at the side of Jyelle's face, I shook my head and knew I was a damn fool for ever getting involved with her ass. I loved her like a fat kid loved cake, though, no lie. Shorty was bad as fuck.

She had skin the color of cinnamon and always wore a long jet-black weave. Her lips were thick and always covered in a pink lipstick. Her eyes were always low from the trees we blew back daily, and shawty's bad was something that was unmatched even after three kids. Even with how A-1 Jyelle's looks were, sometimes I wondered if that was all I had fallen in love with. A nigga like me had an image to upkeep, and Jy was always perfect on my arm. No matter where we went, niggas and bitches eyed her up and down. Niggas envied me for having a dime piece like her while chicks always wondered if the curves she possessed were homegrown, or surgically enhanced.

"I can't believe you really believe this bitch!" Jyelle screamed when I pulled into a WalGreens parking lot.

"Aye, shut the fuck up! When have you known CoCo to ever lie?" I asked her, as I found a parking spot right near the door.

"I swear that hoe can tell you anything and you going for it! You always taking that hoe's side over me! You really think I would bring a kid home that's not yours and not tell you about it!"

"Shittttt, we about to see. Be right back," I told Jy before I hopped out the Lamb and rushed inside of the store.

I felt like I was walking through a haze, while everything around me seemed to be a blur as I searched for the DNA kits. I needed three of them...well shit six of them so I could send them off to two different labs just to be sure my results were accurate.

I found the kits near the pharmacy and snatched up their whole supply. Rushing back to the front to check out, I had the cashier get me a box of gars and gave her close to $300 for everything. Soon as I walked out, I caught how Jyelle tried to discreetly wipe the tears away from her face. Seeing that shit had me feeling anxious and wondering what this hoe was really hiding from me. I had never had a reason to think shawty was doing a nigga dirty, but I guess a sneaky hoe was always full of tricks.

"What you crying for?" I asked Jyelle once I had pulled away from the store and headed down the long road that led to our home.

"Cause...I'm just aggravated that's all," Jyelle told me, and I noticed how quickly her tone had switched up. She had that baby, whiny voice on now. The one she always used when she wanted to persuade me into doing something. "I was just mad about losing our baby. I shouldn't have ever gone and taken it out on CoCo. Just felt like you was sleeping with her again."

"You always feel like somebody sleeping with CoCo. I guess that's your guilty conscience speaking."

"Whatever, Goat, let me be quiet."

"Right. Let's go in here and swab these kids up," I suggested, and she made a clicking tongue with her teeth before crossing her arms over her chest.

"So, how we supposed to explain this to them? To my mama?" Jy stubbornly asked, and I shrugged.

"We don't gotta tell them what it's for. But nothing is gonna stop it from happening."

9

MAINO

"Mmmh, right there, Maino. Yessss, daddy," she yelled, as I tried to murder the pussy.

I was going deep as shit and her ass was tossing it back like it wasn't nothing. Smacking her ass hard as hell, I spread her cheeks and dug as deep as I could finally causing her to have no come back. She tried to tighten her pussy around my dick, and I grunted down and gritted my bottom lip feeling like I was about to nut.

"Shit you're about to make me come," she crooned and I smacked her ass again.

"Come then. I'mma come with your ass."

"Fuck, Maino!" she screamed as I went in and out of her.

"Fuck, Maino, what?"

"This dick is sooo gooood! Shit...I'm coming. I'm coming," she moaned as her pussy felt like it throbbed against my dick.

"Damn baby," I told her before I stroked inside of her faster and harder.

"Mmmmghhhh! Shit!"

"I'm about to nut. Shitttt."

Soon as I felt that build-up on the tip, I pulled back and allowed my seeds to shoot on the inside of the condom. I sat back on the bed and sucked in a deep breath before letting it all out again. Looking over at her, I chuckled when it looked like she was about to go to sleep by the way she had balled up in bed.

"You ain't gon' go wash your stanking ass," I told her, and she chuckled.

"In a minute. I'm still high off the weed and that nut. But don't be tryna play me talking about my ass stank. You wasn't saying that just a minute ago when you had your tongue down my asshole," Sam said and I smacked her ass.

"Tongue wasn't nowhere near your ass girl. You wish," I cracked before hopping up and going into the bathroom.

I quickly dropped the condom into the toilet, making sure I watched that bitch flush away before I walked away. I wasn't tryna have no fuck-ups like I did the last time and allow a bitch to be able run and tell my girl that she was carrying my seed.

Yea I know, I should've kept my dick in my pants after the last time too, but shit Sam was another bad bitch that I just couldn't deny. She wanted a nigga bad, just like Eve had wanted me. I told myself I wasn't going to even mix business with personal again either, but Sam and Eve was way different. Sam was a hood bitch that moved dope and being I had been fucking with this crack rock more than ever before, a chick like her had come in handy. She had a mean ass whip game and cooked some of the best dope in the city. So, in this case, business and pleasure was a must that it was mixed. I kept shawty dicked down as long as it meant she was gon cook that fye ass product for a nigga.

"Move big head," Sam said just as I had climbed into the shower.

I turned the water on and stood back waiting for that shit to heat up. She walked over to me, making small kisses on my chest before looking up at me and smiling. I looked into her brown cat-like eyes, before I winked at her and then grabbed my towel that I had left here the night before. Using the Dove Soap, I lathered it up, and started to wash myself off while Sam kept kissing on a nigga.

"I really like you, Maino. Don't mean anything...just saying," she told me, and I nodded, but didn't say anything.

"The kid just a likeable ass nigga," I chuckled and she mushed me before she got on the tips of her toes to kiss me.

"So, you saying you don't like me?" Sam asked, her eyes scanning over me as she waited for me to answer her.

Seems like this was always how it went. It was always fun and games until feelings got involved. Sam knew just like I told every chick I ever stepped out with that I had a girl and kids at home that I wasn't leaving for nobody. I never got into bed with a female telling them that I was gon' love them and that we was gon' be more than just a fuck thang, and it never stopped them from pulling feelings out their ass and expecting me to feel the same way. Sam was cool. She was probably cooler than Eve was but that was just as far as things went with us.

"I ain't said nothing like that. You cool as shit, Sam, and you know that," I told her, and she nodded before she gave me her back.

I watched as she took her loofah and filled it up with soap, then started to scrub her cinnamon brown skin. Her figure was the shape of a Coke bottle for real. She had a small waist, wide hips, and an ass that looked like two cantaloupes sitting side by side. She was only 5'5 so that shit looked good as shit on her too.

"There you go getting an attitude and shit man. I thought we was gon' be able to kick it for the rest of the night, but you tripping," I told her as I brushed past her and allowed the water from the shower to wash the suds away.

"I ain't tripping at all. I know what it is, Maino. You told me. My fault for thinking that we can at least like each other. But cool," Sam spat, and I nodded before getting out the shower.

I grabbed up a dry towel and dried off my body before going back into Sam's bedroom. She had a condo in Buckhead that had a nice little view of downtown. Even though shawty was hood as fuck, she was smart as hell. She made her money and got out the way, knowing muthafuckas would hate you and try to bring you down if you stayed behind.

I dressed in the same clothes that I had come over in and grabbed my keys and cell phone trying to leave before Sam got out the shower. I would give her some time to get herself together before I came back through and fucked with her again.

After leaving Sam's condo, I caught the elevator to the parking garage and got inside of my new white on white Range Rover. Shit looked like the cocaine that I moved, from the outside all the way to the inside. I had to get rid of everything that I had before, including the house I lived in, every car I drove, and shit even had to change my appearance up. It was all new everything.

I now had a goatee that fell into a full beard. My hair had grown out within the last couple of months and Toya had been twisting it up for me so that it could eventually lock and grow into some dreads. Ever since shit happened with Eve, nothing was the same for me and I knew that it never would be. That was probably the biggest mistake I had made in my life, but shawty had fucked up going after my sister. I could forgive the crazy ass calls to Toya, but when she had told me that she'd put a hit out on my little one, all logic had gone out the window. If I could go back and do shit differently, I definitely would've thought it out and taken shawty out another way, especially if I had known that she was pregnant. I didn't find that out until weeks later when Eve's father sent Mario after me. They claimed that knew without a doubt that I was the father and that I had killed Eve to keep her from telling my girl. Even though it wasn't like what they thought, I made sure that I immediately got Toya and my kids and moved around.

My best bet was to get the fuck up outta Atlanta, but my family being here was the only reason I stuck around. My pops told me he was good, but truthfully, the one thing holding me back was Poe. I knew that she was mad considering she hadn't reached out to any of us since everything had gone down. She had completely distanced herself and nobody even knew if she was safe or not. Every day I didn't speak to her felt like a piece of me was fading away. I hated that Lyric had done everything she did, but it wasn't like Poe wasn't wilding out too. Her fucking with that nigga Ahmeen was treachery at its finest, but some shit I was willing to deal with just to have my sister back.

It took only ten minutes to get to the new spot that I had recently moved my family too. It was a gated community that I knew rapper TI lived in, plus a few other celebrities. One thing that made me choose here to come was the fact that the guards wouldn't let anyone in that wasn't on your visitor's list. Plus, they would always call you if someone was here trying to get in that you hadn't listed. I needed the extra security measure on top of what I already had. Nigga wasn't trying have no pop-ups and for nobody to be able to catch me slipping again.

Once I pulled through the security gates, it took about three minutes to get through the neighborhood and to my house. I pressed the button to open the garage and pulled the Range on the inside. I then walked out to the mailbox to grab the mail. Everything inside was mainly sales papers and magazines, and I started to ball all of it up and toss it until a sticky note sitting on top of one of the letters caught my eye. I looked around before reading it:

Eve. Eve. Eve. Eve. Eve.

I sucked my teeth and then balled the sticky note up before tossing it in the garbage that was on the side of my house. Checking my surroundings, I then went inside and went looking for Toya. The girls were out of town with her people and wasn't due to come back for another few days. Toya was four months along with another set of damn twins and had been put on bed rest so all her ass did was sit around watching TV and eating up some shit.

I took the stairs two at a time and then made my way to the master bedroom. Toya was sitting in the recliner with her eyes glued to the TV while doing some shit to her hair. I laughed and shook my head before pulling my shirt off and tossing it to the floor.

"Nigga, pick that shit up. You get mad at me for going against doctor's order, but your ass won't help keep clean around here," Toya fussed and I chuckled before I grabbed my shirt up and walked over to her.

I kissed her lips and she drew back and looked at me oddly. For a moment, she sat there like she was trying to figure something out while I hoped like hell I ain't smell like no strawberries or shit like that. I always made sure whenever I was out doing my dirt that I took a shower in some regular smelling soap so it wouldn't be no issues.

"What you look at my like that for?" I asked her and she shrugged her shoulders and shook her head.

"No reason. You in for the night?"

"Yea...think I'mma chill out for the next couple of days. Spend some time with you. Feel like I been neglecting you a little bit."

"Yea, just a little bit. You know it gets lonely as hell when the kids ain't here."

"I know, but it's good cause you need that break. Gon' fuck around and be in the hospital and we don't need that."

"Not at all."

"Aye, did anybody come by here today?" I asked, thinking about the note that I had seen.

"No...nobody came by. You know I would've told you if someone did. You expecting someone?" Toya asked as she went back to doing her hair.

"Nah just asked," I told her and grabbed a wife beater and a pair of boxer shorts from my drawer.

I came out the rest of my clothes and then dressed in what I had planned to lounge in for the night. The note was on my mind heavy and considering the shit had Eve's name written all over it, I knew that the fuckin' Cartel had found me. I really was hoping that moving and laying as low as possible was going to work, but I see that if I really wanted to get away, I was gon either have to go after Mario and his pops or leave the city.

I went downstairs to make sure that everything was locked up. I checked every window. The garage door, the backdoor, the basement and shit even went back upstairs to check those windows too. Just before I went back into the room to chill out with Toya for the night, I walked over to the alarm keypad that was on the wall in the middle of the hall. I set the alarm and turned to leave when I spotted a sticky note on the side of a vase that Toya had decorating the hallway.

I snatched it off and sucked my teeth when I noticed that it had the same damn writing as the first one. Either somebody had been in my fuckin' house or Toya was playing with me and thinking this shit was funny. Her ass had literally just gotten over the fact that I fucked with Eve and had finally stopped throwing the shit in my face every time we'd had an argument. She was petty like that so I wouldn't put nothing past, especially being she had a lot of time on her hands.

"Aye, you sure nobody came to the house?" I asked Toya and she shook her head.

"Ohhhhh... damn it, I forgot baby. The A/C people came by, but you should know that. They said that you called them out here," Toya said, and I frowned.

"I didn't call nobody out here. Ain't shit wrong with the A/C. Why the hell you didn't tell me?"

"Because I thought you sent them. Why, what happened?"

"Nothing," I told her and looked down at the sticky note again.

Christmas Eve is approaching

Crumbling the note up, I did another thorough inspection of the house before retiring for the night. I knew for sure that I was sleeping with a burner under the pillow and my rifle right beside me. I promise on everything I love I would never get caught slipping again.

10

POETIC

Days later...

> You ain't the only one
> Who can turn your phone off
> Baby I know how to press ignore
> I won't be crying anymore.

The steam from the shower had the entire bathroom foggy while I sat on top of the bathroom cabinet with a towel wrapped around my body. The tip of a blunt hung from my mouth while I scrolled through every single message that was in this damn phone. Every now and then, I sung the lyrics to Tammy Rivera's track **Only One** loud as hell so that I could be heard from outside of the door. I was being petty as fuck because I knew that Ahmeen was in the bedroom getting ready and could hear me. He had been said over ten minutes ago that he'd needed to come inside to shower, but fuck him, I was busy.

"Aye, Poe, have you seen my phone?" Ahmeen asked, while rattling the doorknob.

"No...why would I have seen your phone? That's your shit," I told him, while clicking on the messages between him and Kiani. I had saved her for last. "Check downstairs in the kitchen."

"Can you hurry up? I gotta shower and be to court in an hour," he yelled, and I shrugged.

"This ain't the only bathroom in the house. I'm busy."

I turned the music up louder before taking another long drag off the weed. I said that after having my baby I wasn't going to smoke anymore, but that was when I had planned on breastfeeding. I had tried that shit and failed and thank God I had, because marijuana had been my solace.

I was trying my hardest to just let this Kiani shit go. Let the fact that they had a baby that I knew nothing about go, but nah. I was still angry, and it still hurt days later. The more I thought about how much he'd lied and how long he'd lied, the more I found every reason to believe he'd been lying about other shit. I had been trying to get to this nigga's phone for days, but he always kept it tucked right under his pillow when he was sleep or on his body when he was mobile. Last night, I made sure to get real nasty with him, make him think that everything was straight so that he could be at ease. Soon as I heard his ass snoring, I eased his phone from underneath him and waited until it was time to get ready to use it.

I had almost given up going through his shit, feeling like somewhat of a fool until I had scrolled up to a huge paragraph that Kiani had sent to Ahmeen. My heart seemed to skip a beat as I read over it quickly, skipping over the parts that I felt had no meaning.

Kiani: *Why would you sleep with me when I told you that I was pregnant and three more times after that if you were just going to stay with that girl? I'm tired of you playing with my feelings Ahmeen. I've been asking you over and over again if we could work on us and be a family and you always say that you would think about it, but never get back to me. You made a complete fool of me at the courthouse, got me looking like I'm some bitter side chick or something. When was you going to tell me that you had a* *baby with her and why the hell didn't she know about Ahmeen? I'm tired of this. You told me you loved us and this is how you treat us.*

"Fuck she mean sleep with her? Loved us? What the hell?" I asked myself as I kept scrolling back through the messages.

Kiani: *Can you come see us? Please?*

    Ahmeen: *Later Ki.*

    Kiani: *I love you so much Ahmeen. you don't even understand.*

    Kiani: *Can we please work things out and be a family? Me and your son almost lost you. I need you Ahmeen. I've been working hard as hell staying clean and doing what I gotta do. Why won't you just forgive me and come back to me baby? I know that you love me and not her.*

    Ahmeen: *I'll think about Ki. Stop hitting my line right now man. Poe looking at me crazy right now.*

"Yo, Poe, open the fuckin' door!" Ahmeen yelled and I sucked my teeth before I slammed his phone down on the cabinet causing the screen to shatter.

I hopped down off the cabinet and dropped the blunt into the sink. Taking in a deep breath, I let it all out and walked over to the door and unlocked it. Ahmeen stood on the other side, his face twisted up into a frown while he looked me over. I took his broken phone and shoved it into his naked chest.

"Take your shit," I told him and pushed past him.

"So, you went through my phone?" he asked me, and I shrugged before I rushed to the closet.

"Fuck you and your phone?"

"You being real disrespectful right now man. You know I gotta lot shit on my plate Poe and I don't wanna flip out on your ass wrong cause the way you coming at me right now."

"Right, let me just get me and Ahmeen... I mean, should we call him Ahmeen. You know since it's another little boy out there with the same exact name as him," I spat and jerked a dress off the hanger.

"Mannnnn..." Ahmeen drawled and sighed.

He ran his hand down his face before he looked down at his

broken phone. I chuckled at his facial expression and then allowed the towel to drop to the floor so that I could get dressed. I pulled the dress up over my thighs and reached behind me to pull the zipper up.

"I told you a hundred times man that I was sorry," Ahmeen pathetically said.

"Yea...I know," I shrugged. "I am too."

"What's that supposed to mean?" he asked me, and I glared at him while tears burned the corners of my eyes. "Why you gotta do this shit right now, Poe? I got forty-five minutes to be at court. These muthafuckas might convict me for this shit. I could go to jail for the rest of my life and you wanna fight with me about a bitch I don't give two fucks about!"

"I hope they do convict your dog ass! Lying ass nigga! You ain't shit, Ahmeen, I swear to God, you gonna regret the moment you ever hurt me," I promised him, as I sucked my teeth.

"A'ight...I'mma just take this as you still mad and let you have that. Let me take a shower and hurry up and get out of here," Ahmeen said as he turned to walk away. Suddenly, he took his phone and chunked it hard as hell into the wall. "Fuck!"

The moment he closed the bathroom door, the tears I was holding back rushed down my face. I quickly ran to the closet to grab the bag that I had packed and hidden for when I got the guts to actually do this. I also grabbed a pair of yoga pants and slid them under the dress I was wearing and then quickly put on a pair of tennis shoes.

Looking around the room, I rushed over to where Jr.'s bag was and grabbed it up along with my phone and purse. My heart was beating a mile a minute as my body heated up from fearing that I would get caught before I could get away. I hated to do this, but I wasn't about to sit back and allow Ahmeen to think that he could just lie to me and get away with it. He'd played me so bad and all he had was a bunch of sorry's like that was just supposed to fix everything that was wrong. He would never let me get away with doing him like this, so I wasn't going to give him a pass either.

I gently grabbed Little Ahmeen out of his bassinet and cradled him against my chest as I quietly left out of the room.

I was down the stairs within seconds and headed down the hall that led to the basement. I knew that from watching the guards that none of them stayed near the backdoor that was down there. They would only check it sporadically, so I took that route as my escape.

I knew that when Ahmeen came out of the shower and saw that I was gone, everyone was getting fired, but I didn't care. If he thought that I was going to be a dumb bitch and sit by while he betrayed me then he had me fucked up. I wasn't one of those low self-esteem having girls that felt like I needed a nigga to breathe. My daddy was a boss ass nigga and not one time did I ever see him mistreat my mama, so there was no way I was going to tolerate anything less than what he had shown me. Ahmeen had better recognize who he was fucking with.

Knock! Knock! Knock!

I knocked on the door and then sighed when Ahmeen called my phone for about the twentieth time since I had left. Looking around nervously, I stood on the outside anxious as hell while I waited for someone to open up. This damn baby was heavy as hell, and I left so fast that I didn't even think to grab a stroller or a car seat. I was only trying to get away as quickly as I could and didn't think about anything other than that. I already had to run across that big ass field that led to the road near the house and then walk for what felt like miles before I could call an Uber.

Leaving in my car wasn't even an option, cause Meen's goon squad wasn't going to do shit but stop me. They would act like they wanted to have a conversation while they low-key checked with Meen to see if I was allowed to leave or not.

"Poetic?" ShaToya asked as she looked me over strangely.

She looked over my shoulder before looking around and then embracing me. Once she pulled back to scan over me, I saw the tear that fell from her eye before she smiled big, and then allowed me to come inside.

"Girl...what in the world? When did you have the baby?" she asked me as we stood inside of the foyer.

"He's almost six weeks old now," I told her, looking around their new place. "How long have y'all been here?"

"Girl, about four months now. Maino came home one day and said we had outgrown the last place and was like leave everything and let's go. Have you talked to him? He didn't even tell me that you were coming by," she said.

"No...I haven't talked to Maino. I tried calling him yesterday, but I hung up when he answered. I don't know. Just got nervous."

"Whyyyyyyy? He says almost every day that he wishes he could talk to you or wish he knew where you were. Oh, my God, let me call him, Poe. He's going to be so happy that you are here," Toya said before she turned around to walk away.

I followed behind her until she stepped inside of the living room. It was a huge open space with modern styled furniture and a huge TV that sat on the wall. I walked over to the sofa and sat down in the corner of it. My feet were killing me, and I felt like I hadn't had a chance to take a deep breath before I ran off. For a good five minutes, I just sat there staring at my son, and telling myself how thankful I should be and how I had needed to get every thought that I wasn't good enough out of my head. It was crazy how you could do everything right and a nigga could have you questioning everything about yourself.

"He said he's on his way and to not leave..." ShaToya said as she appeared in front of me.

"Okay..." was all I said before I laid Ahmeen on top of a blanket next to me.

I unwrapped him and checked his diaper to see if he was wet. He immediately brought his hand up to his mouth and started sucking it. I laughed because that was all his fat ass did was eat. I was already having to put cereal in his bottle to keep him full because had I not, he would be eating every hour.

"Oh, my God, Poe, he is gorgeous as hell girl. Look at that choco-late face," ShaToya told me as she kneeled down near the sofa and stared at him. "Girl...he must looks like his father cause only thing he has is your color. I don't see you at all."

"Yea...he looks like that nigga," I told her and rolled my eyes.

I quickly changed his pamper and redressed him before I pulled a bottle from out of his bag. I used a bottle of Aquafina water I had to pour inside of the powder milk and then shook it up until I could no longer see any flakes. Wrapping the blanket back around Ahmeen, I got ready to take him into my arms when Shatoya held her arms out.

"Can I?" she asked, and I nodded eagerly.

"Yes, girl, go ahead," I told her and we both chuckled as she picked him up and started to feed him. "Where are the twins at?"

"Girl my mama and daddy have them for the week. They took them to Disney World, and being I am pregnant and been having complications, they felt like I needed to stay at home. So I took this as a time to relax, you know."

"Awwwww, y'all gonna have another one?" I said, looking down at her stomach."

"Another two. Twins again. Maino's ass has that gene strong as hell as if he was a twin," ShaToya said and shook her head.

"Well, I'm happy as hell that I don't have it. I don't know what I would do if it was two of him. He's enough," I told her and she nodded knowingly just as my phone rung again.

"Yea," I decided to answer being that I had made it safely away from the house.

"Where the fuck are you?" Ahmeen yelled and I stood to my feet and walked into the hallway.

"We're fine," I told him and could hear him roughly scratching his head.

"Why the fuck you doing this, Poe? You know I said fuck court right? You want a nigga to go jail, so fuck it, but I betcha I'mma find your ass and bring you the fuck home."

"Why would you skip court? Are you crazy?"

"We finna find out. Since you wanna play with me," Ahmeen said, crazily and I sucked my teeth and rolled my eyes.

"Nigga, ain't nobody playing with you. I'm done with your ass. You was telling your other baby mama that you wanted to be with her, so go be with that bitch. Go be with your family nigga, don't let me hold you up," I said, and hung up the phone.

I quickly went to the contact info and scrolled down to where it read *Block this Caller* and clicked it. Locking my phone, I got ready to head back to the living room when the door came open and Maino walked in. My heart dropped when I saw him. He looked so good, and the smile that covered my lips couldn't be hidden when I took off running towards him. I felt like a kid as I jumped into his arms and hugged him tightly.

"Yoooo," Maino said, his voice cracking as he held onto me. "Man, Poe...I missed you so much."

"I missed you, too, Emmanuel," I said to him, tears cascading down my face, as I rested my head against his chest like I used to do when I was a kid.

After what felt like an eternity, Maino placed me down on the floor and gazed his tear-filled eyes over me. I knew he was trying to see if I was okay and why I had just popped up over here unannounced. I had tried calling him from a private number, but when he answered, I had lost my gut and just hung up. I knew if I told him what was going on, it would only cause more problems and me being mad at Ahmeen didn't change the fact that we still had a kid together. I would never take his baby away from him, just myself.

"Damn, you good, ma? It feels like it's been forever," Maino said, and I nodded as he grabbed my hand and pulled me toward the living room.

"It has been forever. I'm sorry...I know I should've reached out before, but I was mad at the world after Lyric...you know," I said, and he nodded.

"Understood. We all was mad at Lyric, but glad we eventually got it cleared up. I tried apologizing a thousand times. I should've never let that girl lie to us like that, but you know situations was happening left and right and it was hard to know what to believe."

"I know..."

"Damn...this you right here?" Maino said looking down at my baby.

"Yea...that's your nephew," I told him, and he smiled.

"Looking just like that nigga. Damn, he cursed the kid."

I chuckled and sat down in the same place as before on the sofa when ShaToya stood up and placed Ahmeen in Maino's arms. I watched on with a huge smile on my face as he looked at my child so lovingly. It caused my heart to melt seeing that he didn't try to act funny with his nephew although he had issues with his father.

After Maino had gotten the baby fed, burped, and asleep, he took him into the girls' room. He then fixed himself a glass of Henny and sparked up some weed. I had never smoked with my brother ever in life and never thought that I would, but it was good that he allowed me to be me around him. We all sat back catching up on each other's lives, neither of us bringing up the past, which was a good thing. I didn't want to talk about what I had done wrong or what I felt like Maino had done wrong. That would only hinder us from moving forward.

It seemed like hours had gone by and I didn't want to leave. I was having so much fun with Maino and ShaToya that I felt like this was where I was supposed to be. Maino told me that I could stay with them, and I wanted to take him up on that offer, but I couldn't lie and say that I didn't suddenly feel bad. What if me leaving had caused issues with Meen's trial and they sent him to jail for it. I didn't really mean it when I told him that I hoped that they convicted him. I was just mad and hurt and speaking off emotions. It would kill me if he got locked up and my baby needed his father.

Ding Dong! Ding Dong!

"Who the hell is that?" Maino asked, hopping up from his seat.

He grabbed the remote to the television and pressed a few buttons causing the security cameras to come up. When I saw Ahmeen standing at the door with his goon squad not far behind him, my heart dropped. He would always joke in the past that if I ever tried to get away from him that there wasn't a place that I could go that he wouldn't find me. I used to laugh and always say *whatever boy*, but now I didn't find shit funny.

"I didn't tell him your address," I told Maino, truthfully, as he looked at me.

"What's going on that he felt the need to come to my house with an army of niggas, Poe?" Maino asked and I sighed.

"Nothing like that. I just wanted to get away for a while, and I missed you. Seriously," I lied, my eyes narrowing in on the cameras.

Ding Dong! Ding Dong! Ding Dong!

Maino walked over to the fireplace and grabbed a big ass gun that I didn't even see sitting there until now. I immediately felt bad as shit as my head dropped into my hands. I never wanted this to happen, but I guess I should've known better when dealing with these two. Maino was a killer for real for real, and Ahmeen was just as Gangsta, not afraid to lose his life for what he believed in. I knew that he believed in him and I, because he often told me. But damn, none of this would be happening had he kept it 100 with me and not tried to play me. I didn't do anything wrong.

"Maino...let me get the door. I don't want y'all fighting. I'm so tired of not being able to co-exist, so please," I urged as I ran behind him.

"You know what, only because I don't want it to get to the point to where you feel like you can't come back around. Go ahead, but if that nigga be on bullshit, I'mma burn his ass," Maino promised, and I nodded knowing he was serious.

I walked towards the door and rubbed my hands against my pants to wipe away the perspiration that had formed. Swallowing back the lump in my throat, I reached for the door, unlocked it and slowly pulled it open. Ahmeen stood there with a more than angry look on his face. His eyes were low, and I knew he was good and high. He sucked his diamond filled teeth and then ran his hand over his nose ring.

"Where my child at?" Meen asked, and I didn't say anything. I crossed my arms over my chest and leaned against the doorway. "You don't hear me fucking talking to you?"

"...he's fine. He's asleep," I said, realizing it was best to not make him angry.

"Go get him and let's go," Meen ordered and I frowned and shook my head.

"I'm staying here," I told him.

"Why the fuck you wanna play with me right now? I been out here looking for your muthafuckin' ass all got damn day while I was supposed to be in court. Your ass better be lucky my attorney was able to get the shit right or otherwise I would be locked up right now, but oh yea, that's what you want right?"

I shook my head as tears began to fall down my face. I was stuck because I knew that it wouldn't be long before Maino came and got in the middle. I was trying my hardest to hold my ground and let Ahmeen know that I wasn't going for his bullshit. I really was done with his ass and it was nothing that he could do to change that.

"Poe...go get my son, and let's go."

"I told you that I'm staying here."

Before I could even react, Ahmeen snatched me up by my neck and pushed me into the door. My body caused a loud bang and I cried knowing that this was it. Out of the corner of my eye, I could see Maino rounding the corner and coming towards us.

"Okay...okay, I'mma come home. I'mma go get him and come home," I told him, desperation evident in my tone.

"Aye, get your hands off her nigga! She said she was staying here!" Maino yelled, and Ahmeen let me go and rushed him.

"Noooooo!" I screamed when the two of them started fighting.

Every last one of Ahmeen's goons ran past me and at my brother. I covered my mouth and backed away, mad that I had put Maino in the situation. Tears rushed down my face as he did his best to fight off the men that were on him.

"Oh, my God! Get off of him," ShaToya screamed as she ran towards them and started swinging.

I couldn't just stand by and watch everything unfold, so I ran into the living room where I knew Maino had left that big ass gun. Looking around, I quickly spotted it leaning up against the side of the sofa. Grabbing, I looked on the side of it, pulled the safety off and then ran to the hallway where the confrontation was still going strong.

POW!

Everybody froze, accept for Meen's men. They had quickly pulled out there guns trying to see where the shot had come from. I could barely hold onto this big ass gun, but I was doing my best. I wanted everyone to see that I was serious. I wasn't going to shoot Meen, but if he didn't call his dogs off my fuckin' brother, I would do my best to shoot their asses until he did.

"You better get them niggas the fuck up outta here," I told Meen and he looked at him with devastation in his eyes.

"Man these niggas is trained to go. You think you holding that gon stop them. Soon as you get my child and get your ass in the car then we all can be gone," Ahmeen barked angrily.

"I ain't going nowhere. You think you finna treat me like I'm some nothing ass bitch then you got me fucked up. I ain't never did shit to you to deserve what you did to me," I told him, getting just as angry that he had the audacity.

"Go find my son," Ahmeen said to Latrel, and he ran off like the do-boy that he was.

When Maino tried to move, one of the other goons, Mark, quickly put a pistol to his head. I aimed the shotgun that I was holding toward Mark and pulled the trigger. I missed him, but I think everyone clearly got the picture that I wasn't playing no games.

"Get that gun away from my brother," I screamed, my entire body shaking.

"Got him boss," Latrel said from behind me.

I glared over my shoulder and saw that he had Little Ahmeen in his arms. Tears spilled from my face, mad that Meen was making things so difficult. All I need was time and my space, but he was acting like that was illegal.

"Don't..." I protested as Latrel handed Little Ahmeen over to his father.

"Don't what..." Ahmeen said as he brought his son up to his face and kissed his cheek. "It's cool. You can stay, but you crazy if you think you gon' take my fuckin' son away from me."

"Ahmeen no..." I said, suddenly breaking down.

"Let's go," Meen told his men and they all left, leaving behind another tragic situation that I was sure I couldn't fix.

11

AHMEEN

Soon as Latrel pulled up to the house, I noticed a black car sitting in my driveway that I didn't recognize. Seems like I was about to fire every last one of my security. I had already put two bullets in the nigga that was supposed to be guarding the door that Poe had left out of earlier. He was a young nigga that I had tried to give an opportunity, but his ass spent too much time on the basketball court rather than doing his fucking job. I was sure he was regretting every moment of that now that he had two slugs in his ass.

"Aye, keep him out here and don't get out until I figure out what's going on. Shit go bad then you take my child to my pops," I told Latrel and slowly got out of the car.

Soon as I stepped out, the doors to a black Lexus opened up, and I immediately spotted Javier, head of the Mexican Cartel. Every man behind me cocked their pistols as I froze in place not sure what to expect. Normally, his daughter Eve and son Mario would come their way, but I hadn't heard shit from them in a long ass time. I thought that I had finally given up, until I heard that someone had murked baby girl and left her floating in a pool. Whoever it was had done her fine ass dirty, but it was just what she deserved for always running up on a nigga thinking shit was gon' forever be sweet.

Javier and the man that he was with stepped out of the car and both of them held their arms up to let us know they wasn't on no bullshit. I raised my hand to let my men know that they could lower their pistols. Walking closer to Javier, I crossed my arms over my chest and stared at the little, but powerful man that stood in front of me. He came from old money just like my pops did, only I couldn't respect him the same. I didn't like the way he handled business and for that reason, I would never lay down and get with what he wanted. No matter the price tag or how many muthafuckas they sent at me.

"Sup," I said first.

"I wanted to talk to you all about my daughter, Eve. She was killed six months ago. Murdered in cold blood," Javier stated, and I could sense the sadness in his voice.

"I'm sorry to hear that. I've lost people close to me as well, so I definitely know how that feels," I told him, and he nodded.

"Yes. I know. I come in peace. I don't care about your recipe anymore. I don't care about the drug game anymore. I loved Eve. She was the strongest person I knew. No one accepted her, but me and her brother and even though she knew she wasn't liked, she fought to prove how much of the Fuentes blood ran through her body. She was a warrior. She had a great heart and the person responsible for her death, I want them dead. I could easily keep sending my men after him, however, he has disappeared, and I haven't been able to find him. He's a little wiser than I thought, which is what brought me to you. I feel that you and I could benefit from each other," Javier said, with eyes solely on me.

"How you figure?" I asked him.

"Maino...he killed my daughter. She was two months pregnant with his child. We know this because we had DNA performed before she was buried and it came back as a match to him. He should be in jail, but I am no snitch. I rather handle my problems in the streets."

"As you should."

"I hired Maino to get the recipe from you and kill you. He failed... hell we all failed," Javier laughed, but I didn't. He cleared his throat and then looked at me seriously. "There's this girl named Poe...I heard that she..."

"What the fuck you asking me about Poe for?" I grew angry and stepped closer to him.

It was bad enough that this nigga was standing in front of me telling me that he had hired my girl's brother to kill me and now he was bringing her name up. I hated to flip out the way that I had on Poe, but losing her was not an option, and I had told her that time and time again. I loved the fuck outta that girl and had lost my shit when I walked out of the bathroom this morning to see that she was gone.

My head was all the way fucked up that I had really skipped out in the middle of a murder trial to find her. They could've revoked my bail, and locked me up until the end of trial, but I ain't care. I just wanted my girl and my son with me. I didn't feel right with it being no other way. I had grown attached to Poe, and now that my son was here, I had grown a love for him that was indescribable. The way I wanted to protect them was just instinct I guess, which was I had to do everything in my power to stay out of jail.

"My daughter put a hit out on her. For some reason, she felt that this Poe was the one thing that would bring you and Maino to your knees. I wanted to find a way to bring peace between us, drop the hit and allow you to do me a solid for doing so, however my son Mario. He doesn't listen to me. He's very angry about my daughter and he will stop at nothing until the person that is responsible for her death has suffered the same fate. I promise you, I have tried," Javier said and without thinking, I grabbed him and tossed him against the Lexus.

"Don't fuckin' play with me alright. I will murk you and this pussy ass muthafucka you brought with you, and I don't give a fuck about what army you got that will come for me. I will body each and every last one of them. You better let your son know...that if he touch my muthafucking girl, I'mma hang his bitch ass by the balls and burn his pussy ass alive," I warned him through gritted teeth.

I let him go and straighten out his shirt that I had caused to wrinkle when I roughed him up. I grimaced as my eyes narrowed in on his face, letting him know that I meant every word that I had said to him.

"You kill Maino, and he will not bother her." Javier cleared his throat and sighed before he backed away towards his car.

Him and his man got inside of the car and moved out of the way so that they could leave. Soon as they had cleared the driveway, I walked over to the truck that Latrel and my son were in and opened the door.

"You go back over there, and you bring Poe home. I don't give a fuck if you gotta kill everybody in that muthafucka, don't leave without her. Just know your life depends on it," I told him and grabbed Ahmeen's car seat.

I turned around and headed inside of the house, hating that I hadn't just killed that pussy ass nigga Maino earlier, but that would only crush Poe more than I already had. She loved that bitch ass nigga and that was very obvious with the way she had reacted earlier when I popped up. Something happened to Maino and she found out I was behind it, she would never forgive me. It was cool, though, I could just get Goat to handle that nigga.

"Bro...come fuck with me. I got something I need you to handle," I said to him the moment he picked up the phone.

"Say less..." he told me, and I hung up and chilled with my lil one until he arrived.

12

GOAT

The following day....

I was up early as hell, trying to handle some shit before nine when Ahmeen had to be back in court. Everybody had flipped out and started panicking when his ass hadn't shown up yesterday morning. The judge was getting antsy and ready to put out a bench warrant for his arrest, but thanks to Marshall's ass, who had come through in the clutch. He'd had one of his boys that worked for the hospital pretend that Ahmeen had been involved in a car accident and was currently receiving medical attention. The judge saw fit to postpone until today, and I was thankful for that cause I had just received the info I had been waiting for a little over an hour ago.

"There that bitch go right there," Latrel, Meen's head goonie said as he pointed out a very pregnant Chanel.

"Yep...ohhh shit! That bitch Ayesha really came through," I told him, and we both hopped out of the car.

Last night, when I had gone to see what Meen needed. He let me know the real reason he didn't show up in court, and I couldn't do shit but laugh at his ass. I told him from jump that he was dumb ass shit for hiding a whole baby from Poe. Shit, Kiani had gotten pregnant before he had even gotten involved with Poe so it wasn't like she could be mad at that, but the nigga swore up and down he knew he was doing. All night he sat there looking like a sad ass puppy, steadily talking about he couldn't lose his girl. I low-key think the nigga wanted to cry a few times, but was doing his best to hold it all in.

He also let me know about Javier from the Cartel stopping through and how that nigga Mario had a hit out on Poe. In exchange for them dropping it, he had to kill Maino. This shit was so crazy, but shit was really like that in these streets. It was eye for an eye, all day every day. You could never do anything and think that you was gonna get away with it.

I had done so much dirt that I knew that one day, eventually, somebody was gonna come for my ass and there was nothing I could do about it.

I told Meen that I had him, but he should've already known without a doubt that I did. I would take that burden off his back any day, no questions asked. No cap.

"Aye," I said, causing Chanel to jump a little as she pulled a box of doughnuts out of the car.

She turned around to look at me, the smile she wore disappearing when she noticed that it was me. The box that she was holding onto dropped from her hands and hit the ground, causing the doughnuts to roll through the dirt. She tried to run, but I rushed her and grabbed her by the back of her hair.

"Monnnnniiiiii!" she screamed before I had a chance to cover her mouth.

Latrel snatched her keys from her hands and ran up the stairs that led to the old Victorian style home that they now lived in. It was in the country part of Jonesboro that was surrounded by other houses that looked like it or mobile homes. Looking around, I started to grow angry that it was taking Latrel so long to find the damn key to open the door. I was about to give up and tell the muthafucka to kick it in when it swung open and Moni stood in the doorway.

Latrel drew his big fist back and punched Moni so hard in his face that it caused him to fly backwards into the house. He ran in, grabbed Moni up from the floor with me coming in right behind them.

"Sit the fuck down," I told Chanel as I dropped her on the sofa and then went back to close and lock the door.

Her hardheaded ass did exactly the opposite of what I said and tried to take off running again. She tripped, falling on her pregnant stomach and yelled out in pain. I walked over to where she was and pulled her up from the floor, walking her over to where Latrel had sat Moni in one of the kitchen chairs.

"Where the tape at?" I asked Latrel, and he reached into the backpack that he wore and pulled out some duct tape.

We took time tying each of them down to the chairs so that they could not move. I tied Chanel's mouth shut so the bitch wouldn't scream anymore and have us fucked up. We didn't need the hoe to talk no way, so as long as she complied and just sat there, she would be fine.

"Your brother tripped the fuck out man. Had me trying to convince Poe to come home all damn night. You know how long that shit took," Latrel said as he pulled a bag a chips out of his bag and sat on the sofa while we waited for Moni to come to.

"How long nigga?"

"Shittttt, we didn't make it back til like four in the morning. Pussy whipped ass nigga talking about if I didn't get her back home he was gon kill me and he was serious," Latrel said, and we both busted out laughing knowing that he was.

"Brooooo, that nigga really made you drag her home?" I asked him, and he nodded.

"Yep...she slept her ass in the guestroom and left him to take care of the baby. Yo, we were all doing everything to keep from laughing, too. He could barely change the baby pampers right. Call himself trying to flex and take the baby and shit and don't even know what he doing." Latrel laughed.

"Nigga, crazy man. I'm surprised she came home. What you told her to get her to finally come?"

"That Ahmeen was telling everybody that he was gonna kill

himself if she didn't. She didn't believe me at first, but I had that nigga Mike send some messages to my phone acting like it was Meen. She fell for it and said that she was only coming back until after the trial."

"Damnnnnnnn..." I laughed and stood to my feet when Moni finally started to stir.

"Nigga was out cold; I ain't even hit him that hard."

"Shitttttt, look at your big ass hands," I told Latrel as he stuffed his mouth with chips and then looked down at his hand.

"The fuck!" Moni yelled, before he spat blood on the floor.

"Brother...sup nigga. Damnnnnn Master Splinter ass nigga, what's good with you?" I said, and he grimaced.

"Fuck you!" Moni aggressively said, and I nodded.

"Bro, you done enough fucking over folks to do us all some good. Chill out playboy," I told Moni and slid a chair in front of him.

"What the fuck you here for? I did my part so Meen can kiss my ass too."

"Nigga, I never knew you was this damn jealous. That man ain't did shit to you," I told him, and he shrugged.

"You don't know what he did to me. But it don't matter. I did what the fuck I did and I ain't sorry for it. Kill me right here, right now. I don't give a fuck. I knew it was coming one day."

"Nah... I ain't gon kill you. I'mma kill your bitch and your baby though," I promised him, and on cue Latrel hoped to his feet and moved over to Chanel.

"Don't touch her pussy. Be a man and do what you gotta do to me," Moni said, and I chuckled.

"Nah, I'mma tell you what you gon' do. That lil' pussy ass DA Lewis that you was getting all cozy with in the courtroom, I want you to call him and tell him that you recant everything that you said and that you lied to save your ass. Then after that, Latrel is going to take you to Marshall and you let him know that you was coerced by the prosecution to lie on your brother. Tell him that you didn't see Quavo get killed and that you don't know who killed him," Moni laughed, and I nodded at Latrel.

He punched Chanel in her face so hard that you could literally hear her nose breaking. I flinched seeing her shit twist while clotted blood oozed at the bottom of her nostrils. I felt bad as shit cause I ain't like coming for no chick when it involved men, but there was no way I could send Moni to Marshall all bloody and beat up. They would never believe he came in on his own.

"Chanel!" Moni yelled as her head dangled while she tried to keep consciousness.

"So, what's it gon' be, Moni?" I asked him.

"Nigga you can suck my dick," he told me, and I shook my head.

"Bro for real? You gonna let your pride cause your girl to get fucked up?" I asked him and sighed as I nodded at Latrel again.

This time instead of punching her in the face, Latrel went into his bag and pulled a hammer out. My eyes bucked cause even I wasn't expecting that shit. Instead of watching, I took my phone out to look at the time. It was going on 7:30, which meant I had an hour and a half to get this shit handled before Meen's trial started back up.

"Mmmghhhhh!" I heard a muffle cry, and I looked up to see Chanel's chest rising and falling rapidly.

"You niggas some hoes! Some pussy ass niggas!" Moni yelled, and I cocked my head to the side.

"And what are you? Do what the fuck I said, and we'll leave you and your bitch alone," I told him, frustrated as fuck.

I stood up from the chair that I was sitting in, and then walked over towards Chanel myself. I didn't want Latrel's ass to hit her no more cause he'd fuck around and kill the girl. Instead, I drew my hand back and slapped her hard enough that it caused her head to pop sideways.

"We can go all day. It's up to you," I told him, and he sighed. I was hoping the nigga was giving in.

"A'ight...a'ight. Bring me the fucking phone," Moni told me and I nodded. "It's over there on the end table near the window."

I followed his instructions and went and got his phone for him. I then went to my phone and pulled up the number for DA Lewis that I had gotten from Ayesha. I had to really send her a real nice care package. Ever since Ahmeen had told me about her, I stayed on her ass trying to make sure she knew that her secret about her having Moni's baby was only safe if she looked out. She had gotten too comfortable, thinking that we were just gonna let shit ride cause she had a Little Shakur but nah. I had to wake that bitch the fuck up and when I did, she had gotten me all the info I needed to find Moni, and a list of other witnesses that might be detrimental to Ahmeen's case.

"Hello...Yea it's ummm, De'Moni Shakur," he said, his voice shaking as he spoke. "I need to recant my testimony...I made it all up."

"Huh? Are you okay, Mr. Shakur? Is anyone threatening you? Do we need to get someone out to the home?" he asked him, and I could tell he was in the car driving.

I hit the mute button on the phone. "Make that shit sound good nigga," I coerced, and quickly unmuted the phone.

"Nobody is threatening me. I lied, and I'm going to let the DA know that I did too. I'm sorry for wasting your time," Moni grimaced.

"Are you aware that you can go to jail for lying under oath? Your testimony and cooperation is the only thing that is keeping you out of jail. Remember you are facing forty years in prison, Mr. Shakur!" Lewis yelled, and I quickly hit the end button.

"I'mma untie your ass and you gon' fuckin' act right. I'mma be checking with Latrel every five minutes to make sure he good. If he doesn't text me back within a minute, I'm going to assume that shit went wrong and I'mma kill you bitch, no cap," I told him, and he sucked his teeth.

I rushed into the kitchen and grabbed a knife from the cupboard then went back over to De'Moni. It took about three minutes to get the nigga freed from all of the tape that he had around him. He slowly stood to his feet, and we were toe to toe staring each other down for what felt like an eternity. I really wanted to pump this nigga with a whole lot of slugs for the way he was handling shit but knew that I couldn't. Him doing this was the only thing that could have Ahmeen's trial thrown out. This was all they had. They didn't have a gun, or any evidence that Ahmeen was even in the area besides a couple of text messages that he'd sent that had pinged off of cell towers near the warehouse, but that wasn't enough to convict him. Even I knew that.

"I promise you nigga, you gon' feel me," Moni threatened as he walked past me.

Soon as him and Latrel had left out, I went to send Ahmeen a text message to let him know we was almost there. We still had about an hour and ten minutes to go, and we wasn't too far from the city. All Latrel had to do was catch Marshall before he left his office.

Meen: *Almost there. Won't be late.*

I stuffed my phone into my pocket and then walked over to the refrigerator. Pulling it open, I looked around until I spotted a Sprite and some green grapes. Pulling them both out, I sat the soda down on the cabinet and then went to wash the grapes off when I heard a bunch of movement.

Looking to where I had Chanel, I seen her body shaking uncontrollably and thought that she was trying to get away until her head started to jerk all crazy like. I rushed towards where she was and stepped in front of her. Her eyes had rolled into the back of her head and foam was spewing from the sides of the tape.

"Oh shit...." I said, jerking the tape away from her mouth so that she could breathe.

I then looked around for that same knife that I used to free De'Moni with. When I spotted it, I grabbed it from the floor and quickly cut away every piece that bind her to the chair. Her body almost fell over and hit the floor and I grabbed her before she could. She had completely stopped shaking by then and I started to panic thinking that she was dead.

"Chanel! Chanel!" I shook her but didn't get a response.

I gently laid her across the floor and started to feel her wrist for a pulse. I then placed my ear to her mouth to listen for any breathing. I didn't see or feel shit. I didn't know what the fuck to do, so I tried doing CPR even though I ain't know shit about it.

Her chest bounced up and down as I pushed on her over and over again, trying to get some type of response from her, but nothing.

Shawty was dead and no matter how I made it seem in front of Moni, my intentions was to never kill her.

"Fuck," I said, a tear slipping from my eye as I eyed Chanel. "Fuck, man shit."

I stood to my feet and then rushed to wipe off everything me and that nigga Latrel touched. Moni was fucked up for everything he had done and I felt like he had deserved everything that was coming to him, but not this. That was that man's baby, and I could only imagine how fucked up he would be when he walked in and saw this.

"Shit..." I said after checking Chanel once more.

She really fuckin gone, I thought to myself, after I rushed out of the house. I waited until I had made it at least a mile up the road before I called for an Uber to take me away from here. I didn't even have the mind to sit in the courtroom today. This shit had me fucked up that we were put in this position. Shit wasn't supposed to be like this and I swore I would do anything to bring it all back and change the outcome. Wish I had known that Moni felt how he had and maybe I could've done something to make him see that he was tripping. I ain't know how or what I could've done to change it, but if I had known things would've ended up like this then I would've tried hard as hell.

If my muthafuckin' day hadn't been bad enough, the moment my Uber pulled up to the crib, I got an email notification that said it was from IntelliGenetics. I had gone to the lab the next morning after performing the DNA swabs on all three of my kids with Jyelle. They told me to give them 48-72 hours and they would email me the results and also send a mailed copy.

When I opened the email, I carefully scanned my eyes over each result to be sure that I was reading it correctly. The first one I read over was from our oldest child Jy'Asia it said:

Based on the DNA analysis, the alleged Father, Ge'Loni Shakur, cannot be excluded as the biological Father of the Child, Jy'Asia Shakur, because they share genetic markers. Of the genetic identity systems tested, 15 of 15 match. (99.999919312054% of the African-

American male population is excluded from the possibility of being the biological Father).

However, when I scrolled to the next test results it was a totally different outcome:

Based on the DNA analysis, the alleged Father, Ge'Loni Shakur, can be excluded as the biological Father of the Child, Ge'Loni Shakur, Jr, because they do not share genetic markers. Of the genetic identity systems tested, 0 of 15 match. (17.00187290% of the African-American male population is excluded from the possibility of being the biological Father).

Based on the DNA analysis, the alleged Father, Ge'Loni Shakur, can be excluded as the biological Father of the Child, Germaine Shakur, because they do not share genetic markers. Of the genetic identity systems tested, 0 of 15 match. (17.00187290% of the African-American male population is excluded from the possibility of being the biological Father)

"Excuse me sir, is this not the right address?" the Uber driver asked, snapping me out my reverie.

I looked up at him and then remembered that we had pulled up to my house. I sighed and then got out of the car, trying to figure out how I wanted to play this. I could either kill this bitch and toss her ass in the closest lake, or I could just leave the bitch alone and make her suffer for the rest of her life. I ain't know which, but I knew that she had picked the perfect day to fuck with me.

13

DE'MONI

"P reciate it," I told the Uber driver and then climbed out of the car.

I sighed and shook my head as I tried to figure out what the fuck was about to happen to me now. The DA had been calling my phone nonstop since I had hit him up letting him know that I had lied on the stand. He told me that if I didn't call him by 10:30 this morning that he was going to send the sheriffs here to pick me up. It was now a little after 11, and I was hoping me and Chanel had time to bounce. I had saved up a little money in case this was to happen, so I knew that we would be good for a few months wherever we went.

Soon as I walked up the steps that led to the house and noticed the door was slightly open, I froze before looking around. I knew that once that big nigga told Goat that I had done what was asked of me that he wasn't going to be here when I got back. I didn't have a pistol on me or shit to protect myself, but I shook my head and slowly pushed the door open and looked around before going in. I gently closed and locked the door behind me.

I really wanted to get at them niggas bad as hell for the way they had done Chanel, but knew it was best for me to call a spade a spade and just let it go. I had done my dirt and they had done theirs and I knew if I kept it up, it would never stop. Chanel was due to have our baby any day now and I ain't wanna keep putting her through shit. She had already uprooted her entire life, changed her identity up, and had to stop fucking with her family because of me. Seeing how hard she rode for me all these months was enough for me to say fuck it and let them have that.

"Chanel!" I called out and looked around for her.

I rounded the corner that led into the kitchen and when I spotted her sprawled out on the floor, I froze. Her body looked lifeless, but being that I didn't see any blood, I was hoping that she had just fallen asleep or something.

I took in a deep breath and made my way over to where she was. Kneeling down next to her, I grabbed her arm and raised it only for it to fall out of my hand and onto the floor. Her eyes were rolled behind her head and white shit was caked up around her mouth.

I shook her, but when she didn't move, I blinked back tears seeing that she was dead. My hand went to her stomach, and I pressed down on it, hoping that I could feel some movement from my little one. She was supposed to have had our daughter a few days ago, but was over-due, and scheduled to be induced next week.

"Yo...the fuck man?" I said, my heart dropping as tears fell from my eyes. "Chanel?"

Bam! Bam! Bam!

The knocking at the door caused me to jump. I reached towards Chanel and closed the lids of her eyes before gently kissing her lips. Standing to my feet, I rushed towards the bedroom, knocked the mattress over and grabbed the pouch that held the money I had been saving.

Bam! Bam! Bam!

"De'Moni Shakur! Open up! Atlanta Police!"

I turned around and headed towards the back of the house, then pulled down the handle that would let the opening to the attic down. Quickly climbing the stairs, I closed it back and then rushed over to the window that would lead me to the roof of the house. I ducked down and looked around at what I was up against. It was only two police cars and four men. Two were at the front and two at the back. When the two in the front went inside, I quickly slid down the side of the house and took off running as fast as I could.

Just when a nigga was trying to be peaceful and let this shit go, these muthafuckas turned around and took everything that I had left. Now here I was, a menace with nothing to lose. Swear if they thought I had lost my shit, they hadn't seen shit yet.

14

POETIC

Three days later...

I yawned as I sat up in bed and looked around the room. The sun peaked in through the curtains causing my eyes to squint. I shielded my face with my hand then grabbed my phone to see that it was early as fuck. Shaking my head, I swung my legs around and slowly got up and went inside of the bathroom.

I only came home because I didn't want there to be anymore issues between Meen and Maino. Plus, I knew that I needed to be here for the trial. I wasn't trying to have him skipping on more days and doing what was needed of him because I was in my bag right now. I didn't give in to him though, and I was pretty sure he knew that too based off how well I avoided the fuck out of him. I had one of his men move all of my stuff into the downstairs guestroom that we used to sleep in when he'd first been shot. I now had majority of my clothes, my toothbrush, and hair and make-up products with me. I didn't go upstairs for shit, and I made sure to lock my door when I was here. And to make matters even worse, I still had his ass on my block list. Soon as this trial was over, I was giving his ass the deuces and moving on with my life. The more time I spent down here alone, the more I convinced myself that I was doing the right damn thing.

I wished that they had hurried up and gotten this case over with too. A few days ago in court, I didn't know what was going on, but I knew that something had happened that caused the judge to call a recess and to dismiss court almost as soon as it had started. Ahmeen didn't even know when he was supposed to go back, which only meant it was much longer that I was going to be here.

Even though Ahmeen didn't have my number, the nigga had really gone as far as to sending me an email. It was a long ass letter of him telling me again how sorry he was and how he had only told Kiani shit just so she wouldn't get sad and go out and do drugs again. I didn't care about none of that shit. The nigga still shouldn't have lied about their kid and apparently sleep with the bitch while we we're together too.

Eventually, I probably would've grown to accept the fact that he had child. The baby didn't ask to be here and was made prior to me and Ahmeen getting together. It was the cheating and telling Kiani that they could be a family that kept me adamant about things being over with us. He could say all day that Kiani's addiction is what made him feed her lies, but that only meant to me that he was choosing her well-being over mine, and I wasn't about to play second to no one.

I had done that foolishly when I first started messing with Ahmeen, but at the time, I was wilding and living free after Melody's death. Circumstances had changed and if he thought I was going to be some dummy that allowed certain shit because of who he was, then he had the wrong bitch. He could feed Kiani that bullshit cause obviously she was used to it. Not me.

After showering and getting dressed, I snatched up my phone and made my way down the stairs and into the kitchen. Since Ahmeen wanted to play with me and act like he was ready to be a single father, I made sure that I put Little Ahmeen in his bed every night. From all the way down here, I would hear him crying his little eyes out, but not one time did I move to offer any assistance. I just let him figure it out and it seemed like he'd been doing quite fine too.

I thought about making me a bowl of cereal, but the way milk had been messing with my stomach since having Little Ahmeen, I thought better of it. Instead, I popped some bread into the toaster and quickly fried some sausage followed by some eggs.

"You ain't make me none?" Ahmeen asked the moment I had grabbed my plate and sat on a barstool at the kitchen isle.

I rolled my eyes but didn't say anything. Seeing Little Ahmeen had me missing him, but I didn't want to seem pressed and acted as if I was good on the inside. Ahmeen looked over at me as if he was waiting for me to speak, but I buried my head in my plate and savored the flavor of the eggs.

The moment he turned his back to me, I couldn't help but noticed the new tattoo he'd gotten and wondered when he'd had the time to do that. He had my name in big, bold letters across the top of it and I stared for a long while, almost getting caught up in my feelings.

When he turned back around, I quickly dropped my head and went back to eating my food. I could feel Ahmeen getting closer and closer to me, but I refused to give him anymore of my attention. He could buy more purses, shoes, clothes, and get as many tattoos as he wanted, but none of it would change my mind.

"Poe, how much longer you gonna keep this up?" Ahmeen questioned, and I kept chewing.

"Foreva, so stop trying," I told him, seriously.

He chuckled, and I looked up, mad as hell that I did. The nigga looked like new money with the way his fade was neatly shaped up. The scar on his head, made him look like a fucking warrior and his chocolate baby face was all of a sudden making me weak. I noticed how much bigger his chest had gotten and when he brought his glass of orange juice to his lips and his pecs flexed, I slowly swallowed the eggs that were in my mouth. He was holding onto our son like a pro ass pappy and I wanted to smile but had to remember that it was still fuck him.

"I'm about to go downstairs and hit the gym. Do you mind keeping our son?" he asked sarcastically, and I sucked my teeth and held my arms out for my baby. He handed him over to me, and without my permission, leaned over and placed a kiss on my cheek. "Hopefully, when I get done, you'll let me take you out to lunch or something. Been too long since I had time with you, and I miss you," Ahmeen told me before walking away.

I glared at the tattoo again before sighing and finishing up my food. Shaking my head, I told myself over and over again that I was not forgiving him and not allowing him to think that I was some weak bitch. Just the thought of me failing myself caused me to lose my appetite. I pushed my plate away and climbed off the barstool. I brought Little Ahmeen up over my shoulder and walked into the living room so that I could watch some TV.

For whatever reason, all of the blinds were pulled open on the eight-foot-tall windows and caused a lot of light to shine inside of the room. I laid Little Ahmeen down on the sofa and then walked over to where the switch sat on the wall, ready to close every last one of them when I noticed a white truck outside with a red bow on top. Curiosity got the best of me, and I rushed over to grab my son up, before I took him outside with me where the truck sat in the driveway.

"What the hell?" I smirked, noticing that it was a brand-new Bentley Bentayga.

"Both of my babies gotta ride in the best," Ahmeen said from behind me.

I turned around to see him standing there with his hands shoved into his grey sweats. He had a huge smile on his face, and I couldn't even hold back my excitement. Out of everything that Ahmeen had gotten for me, I wouldn't lie and say if this truck didn't make me happy.

"You got this for me?" I asked him, and he nodded.

"Yea...check it out. Brand new 2018, shawty. Shit fresh off the floor."

"Hmmmm," I told him and handed him Little Ahmeen before I rushed over to the car and pulled the door open.

I ran my hands across the fresh peanut butter seats before climbing inside and looking around. I touched just about every button there was, before I turned around to look in the backseat.

Ahmeen had filled it with red and pink balloons, while a dozen of pink roses sat beside a white teddy bear. I reached for the bear when I noticed the black box that was sitting in the middle.

"What is this?" I questioned, before opening the box and revealing one of the prettiest diamond rings I had ever seen.

"What it look like?" Ahmeen asked and I glared up at him.

"Meen..."

He took the box from my hand, and I couldn't stop staring at him. Tears suddenly skipped down my face, and I brought a trembling hand up to cover my mouth. I had to shake my head, because I was fighting so hard to not give in, but how could I not at this point? Fuck all the gifts, Ahmeen was proposing to me, and I was ready to say yes before he even opened his mouth.

"I know I fucked up, but I said that if you gave me another chance, I was going to prove to you how much you meant to me. I ain't about games ma. Since I was a young nigga, I always said that when I met my queen, she would know exactly what it was like to be with a king. I would never make her doubt herself. Never make her feel like she wasn't number one in my life, never make her think she couldn't trust the nigga that said he loved her. I had broken that promise to myself and not only did I fuck up your trust, but I hurt you and I recognize that and never want to see you that way ever again.

I didn't know what it was back then, but when you pulled up drunk, toting a pistol in the hood, I knew me and you was destined for something great. I never thought that in a little over a year later, we would be living in a big ass house and have our first child together, but I'm happy about that and don't want it any other way. Anyway, Poetic...King, I love the fuck outta you girl, and I wanna know if you would please, stop being mad at a nigga, tell me you will marry me, and please give me some pussy?" Ahmeen asked as he dropped down on one knee in front of me while I still sat in the truck. He had the ring in one hand and our son in the other. It was truly a sight to see.

I burst out laughing before I burst into happy tears. Both hands covered my face to hide my embarrassment from the way I was crying right now. It was like all of Meen's goon squad had all eyes on us right now. Some of them were recording while some were watching and smiling damn near as hard as I was.

"Say yes!" Latrel yelled. "That man loves you!"

"Meen...oh, my God," I said, wiping the tears away that had stained my face.

"What that mean?" Ahmeen asked and I looked down at him and shook my head.

"No...I can't," I told him, and I could see that his whole mood had changed.

"Wait did she say no?" I heard Latrel say and I sighed, feeling bad that this was happening for others to see.

"Yo, you serious right now?" Ahmeen asked and I bit at the inside of my lip nervously.

"You hid a baby from me..."

"Mannnn," Ahmeen drawled as he dropped his head. "I told you that I was sorry about keeping Kiani's kid from you a thousand damn times. What else you want me to say?"

"I don't want you to say shit. I don't have time to be trying to figure out what's a truth or a lie when it comes to you. Damn, I don't want it to be like this, but you did this to us. You hurt me so bad and as if things weren't already fucked up in my life, I'm tired and just mentally drained right now," I told him, truthfully causing tears to fall from my eyes.

"Poetic, man don't do this shit," Ahmeen begged.

He turned and waved Latrel over to him. He then placed Ahmeen in his arms and quickly turned back to where I was sitting inside of the truck.

"I'm thinking about going back home. I miss my family..."

"No, the fuck you not, Poe. Like damn, I fuck up one time and you ready to bail out on a nigga. What the fuck is you saying?"

"One time? You fucked Kiani several times according to those text messages and then you telling her you want to be with her. That's not one mistake, that's several, which means at some point it had to be on purpose. I can't get that shit out of my head."

"I didn't mean it when I told her I wanted to be with her. I told you that already. I just tell her what she wants to hear so she can stay clean for that damn baby man. I know you'll never understand that, but..."

"Nah, I don't understand it because I would've never put another nigga's feelings before yours. Maino begged and begged me to either stay with him or to come home. Tears threatening to fall down his face as he sat there listening to me tell him how much I really loved you and how I wanted to be with you, but couldn't understand why you hurt me this way," I told Ahmeen, and he grimaced.

"Man, don't tell me what the fuck your brother said. That nigga gonna say whatever he gotta say to get you away from me. You stupid as fuck if you listen to him."

"But did you hear what *I said*, Meen? You ain't hurt me? Cheating on me with your old bitch and then pretending like you fuckin' love me?"

"I told you why I lied, and I told you why I told Kiani what I told her," Ahmeen barked getting real close to me.

"Right because her feelings mean more to you than mine, right? And I see you never denied sleeping with her. Ughhhhhh, get away from me, Meen. Damn it!" I cried even more, before I pushed him away from me.

I climbed out of the truck and tried to walk around him when he grabbed me and pulled me close to him. He wrapped his arms around me and held onto me for a long while. His warm body felt so good to me, and I felt like it had been forever since I had felt this close to him. It was unfortunate that things had come to this, but I was remaining strong in the way that I felt.

Ahmeen let me go and looked down at me. He used his thumbs to wipe away the tears that stained my face and tried to kiss me again, but I turned my head away. I admit that this was probably the hardest thing that I had ever done in my life, and I really wanted to forgive Ahmeen and get back to loving him, but I couldn't. I was so broken inside.

"I'm sorry," I cried as I looked up at him to see that he was fighting back his tears.

Ahmeen only nodded his head but didn't say anything. When I walked around him to go back inside, I glared over my shoulder to see him pacing back and forth across the driveway. He then drew his arm back and tossed something into the air.

I watched as he hopped into the truck he had gotten me, started the engine and quickly skirted out of the driveway with a few of his men hustling to follow behind him.

"You cold as fuck," Latrell told me, and I shrugged.

"Maybe one day," I said to myself before I went inside and closed the door behind me.

15

MAINO

"Oh, my God, that movie was so freaking good," Toya said as we walked out of the movie theater.

"Yea, that shit was dope as hell. Wakanda Forever. A nigga come busting at me like that, you better be just like ol' girl. Them chicks was the truth," I told her, and she mushed me.

"Shit, I been by your side through it all, haven't I?"

"Yea, you have baby. Thick and thin type shit."

I walked around to Toya's side of the car and opened the door for her. Soon as she got in, I closed the door and went around to the driver's side. We had just finished seeing Black Panther and it had me on some Bonnie and Clyde type shit right now. A nigga was really feeling a lot of appreciation for Toya and had me ready to give up my doggish ways. This damn movie was motivational like a muthafucka. I was all of sudden thinking about peace and black love.

I chuckled at the thought of it before I slid inside of the car and started the engine. I was getting ready to drive off until I noticed a piece of paper tucked underneath the windshield. I opened the door and then reached out to get it before sitting back inside.

"What's that?" Toya asked me as I unfolded the piece of paper and looked down at it.

307 days until Christmas Eve, but will you make it until then?

I crumbled the note up and stuck it in my pocket before I looked around. My eyes narrowed in on everyone that I saw walking around before I veered through the rearview mirror. Reaching beside me, I checked to make sure my burner was still there before backing out of the parking lot.

"Maino...what's wrong? Why you look like you've seen a ghost?" Toya asked me, pulling me from my daze.

"Oh shit...my bad I was just thinking about something."

"What was on that paper?"

"Club advertisement," I lied and drove away.

"You sure you're okay?" Toya asked, and I reached over and grabbed her hand, and kissed the back of it.

"I promise you, I'm good, babe. Just relax," I told her, and she smiled at me before placing her hands over her stomach.

I pulled out of the lot and headed home, careful to keep an eye out to make sure that we wasn't being followed. Apparently, I hadn't been doing a good job of that in the past because whoever the fuck kept leaving these notes was clocking my every move. I was starting to think that whoever it was that was on me, had to be something other than Mexican. Anytime I saw somebody that looked like they could be a part of the cartel or affiliated in some type of way, I moved with extra caution.

This shit was starting to drive me crazy. All this looking over my shoulder and having to change up my whole look was really starting to weigh me down. At this point, I knew that it was time to leave Atlanta behind. I had enough money stashed away that I could easily find somewhere to open up a few business and live life lavishly for the rest of my life. My pops had always made sure that he set every one of his kids up right, not to mention, I got out here and got my own bread.

"Babe, what's the place you was talking about moving to, if we ever moved away from here?" I asked Toya just as I entered the highway.

"Gatlinburg, Tennessee. They got all those mountains up there and some huge cabins, and I just feel like it will be a good place to settle down at when you're done with the life," she told me, and I nodded.

"Bet...I want you to get in contact with a real estate agent and see what you can find us. I've been thinking I'm ready to go. After all that shit that popped off with Poe and her fuck ass nigga, I'm starting to see I need to move around and do something different before I end up in jail or dead," I told Toya, blaming everything on Ahmeen, even though it was partially the truth.

I had been thinking about murking that nigga Ahmeen, but that was a constant thought even before that stunt he pulled when he came to my house. It was probably his bitch ass putting these damn notes on my shit, and I swore on everything I love, if I found out it was, that nigga was as good as dead.

"I really think that's a good idea. Don't think I haven't noticed that you've been on edge a lot over the past few months. I know we didn't just up and move out of the blue for nothing," Toya commented, and I shrugged.

"Right...so check into it, ASAP, and let's go."

~

"What up?" I said, as I walked into Sam's crib and went over to the couch.

She nodded her head before walking away and going inside of the kitchen. Moments later, she came back with a black duffle bag and tossed it at my feet. I chuckled before I glared at her and then down at the bag. Unzipping it, I scanned over the contents and then closed it back.

"You ain't speaking?" I asked Sam, and she shrugged before leaning against her recliner.

"You text and said you was coming to pick your shit up so there you go," she sassed and placed her hands on her hip.

I looked her up and down, my eyes pausing at the triangle that formed between her legs. Her pussy print was on full view and I licked my lips before I shook my head and reminded myself that I was going to stop being a dog.

"You right. Preciate it ma. I put you a little extra in there. You know how I do," I told Sam before I placed an envelope filled with cash on the coffee table.

I stood up to leave and could hear Sam clicking her tongue behind me. As hard as it was to walk away from her and not get a piece of that ass, I was glad that I did. All this shit was happening to me was happening because of me. Had I never jumped into bed with Eve then things probably would've never gone as far as they did. Now here I was getting ready to uproot my family and leave the only home I've ever known. I knew that Sam was far from Eve, but I still wasn't trying to play with her feelings like I had with so many women before her.

"Really hate I ever started fucking with you," Sam said just as I grabbed for the doorknob.

"What?" I turned to face her.

"You heard what I said. I hate that I ever started fucking with you. I should've known better, but it's cool, Maino. I hope you and your baby mama be realllll happy together."

"I apologize," I told her genuinely, before I tugged at my beard. "I'm just a dog ass nigga and I realize that shit. I been fucking over women all my life cause I know I can get away with it. You ain't deserve that shit, and I apologize for fucking with your heart like that."

I walked over to her and pulled her into my chest. I hugged her for a good while then pulled back and placed a kiss on her forehead. Tears dripped from her eyes causing me to feel bad as hell. I swore after this time, I was done with the dumb shit. I just hoped that she would forgive me and allow us to keep getting a bag together.

"Hit me up if you need me," I told Sam, before I turned to leave.

I promise this was the last time.

16

AHMEEN

"Mr. Shakur...and Ms. King, right?" My attorney Marshall said as me and Poe stepped into his office.

"Yep...this is Poetic...the one I been telling you about," I told him, and he chuckled.

"Right. The one you haven't stopped telling me about. You two have a seat. Where's the baby?" he asked, as Poe and I sat down.

"My pops got him until we get done here."

"Ok, ol' grandpa Shakur. He's making me feel like I'm behind and shit. Man I gotta catch up," Marshall chuckled and I did too.

"Nah, these grandkids got that nigga with gray hairs. It'll turn you into an old man quick," I informed him.

"I bet it will. Well, look, like I was telling Tobias before you came down here, I got some good news and I got some bad news. I'm going to give you the good news first because I feel like it'll be a weight off your shoulders," Marshall said, and I sat forward in my seat.

"Give it to me."

"The good news is that all charges against you have been dropped. The judge called for a mistrial. A few days ago, your brother De'Moni came to see me that same day the judge called for that recess. He told me that he was coerced by the DA and that everything that he testified against you wasn't true. He was only saying whatever it was he needed to say so that he didn't have to go to jail," Marshall informed me, and I feigned dumb.

"Yo, for real? So just like that...they dropped the charges?" I asked and he nodded.

"Wow..." Poetic chuckled, relieved, and I glared at her for a good moment. "That's so good."

"Yea, I mean that was really the only leg that they were standing on. No murder weapon and not really any other witnesses to the crime, then there really isn't anything else pointing to you. The DA is going to have to rebuild their case, but I don't see them coming for you about it again," Marshall told me, and I smirked as I sat back in my seat.

"Good," I said and clasped my hands together.

"For that bad news that I have, I just want to put you on alert that De'Moni did leave witness protection. They aren't able to find him, and I really don't know where his head is at. After what y'all told me he did, I'm not sure that he's not going to try you again. You sure you don't want to press charges...I don't trust this son. Not to mention, the police believed he killed his girlfriend that had been in the program with him. She was found dead in their home," Marshall said, and I shook my head and frowned.

"Chanel?" I questioned, and Marshall nodded.

"Yes, still waiting on her cause of death, but her and the baby she was pregnant with passed away."

"What the fuck?" I mumbled, wondering if Goat knew about this.

"Right, which is why I think you need to press charges. He's obviously a monster." Marshall told me and I shook my head.

"Nah, I think we gon' be straight. So, shit, what I need to do? Or am I free free?" I asked, and he chuckled and stood to his feet.

When he held his hand out, I stood to my feet as well and we shook it up.

"You're free my brother, and as always, it was a pleasure working with you and your family. Stay out of trouble and hopefully you don't need me for anything else, but if you do, know that I'm here," Marshall told me as he walked me and Poe out.

We shook hands again before getting onto the elevator and heading back out to the car. I couldn't stop the smile that was on my face knowing that his shit had actually worked. That nigga Goat had really come through for your boy and now I was free to find that nigga Moni and fuck his ass up for even putting me in this position in the first place. For the nigga to kill a pregnant chick was on some next level psycho pussy shit. He just better hope that the police found his ass before I did.

It was time to really get to this money, though. I had one of the biggest shipments of Heroin ever to oversee and now that I didn't have twelve on my back, I could personally see to it that things went right. This was going to be the payday of a lifetime and the first time my brand-new product made its way world-wide at the same time.

"Time to celebrate. I'm throwing a party tonight," I told Poe just as we got inside of her new Bentley truck that I refused to let her ass drive.

I guess you could say that it was my shit because I wasn't letting her get behind the wheel until she accepted my proposal. I couldn't believe she had told me no and was really serious about it. I thought she was playing with a nigga on some petty shit, but Poe's ass was still sleeping in the damn guestroom and still had me up all night with Jr.

I had to give it to her though cause the way she was treating me had me ready to bitch up damn near every night I went to bed without her. This shit was killing a nigga for real, and I swore on everything I loved that I would never lie or fuck another female again. No cap. I ain't never jacked off so much in my damn life. Every night after I got Jr to sleep, my dick was in my hand mad as fuck and having to talk myself out of kicking Poe's door down. Shit was bad and I just wanted to fix it so I never had to go through this hell again.

"Throwing a party where? You ain't even have time to plan. How you expect people to come out at last minute like this?" Poe asked as she scrolled through her phone.

"Trust, the whole fuckin' city gon show up. It don't take nothing but telling a few of the right people. Don't even worry about all that though. Who the fuck you over there texting?" I asked, and she glared up at me.

"You ain't seen me send not one damn text message, so get out my phone eye hustling and shit," Poe spat and rolled her eyes.

"Girl, I'll get your damn phone disconnected you keep playing with me."

Poe laughed before she went back to scrolling through her phone. I glared over at her, and then reached out and ran my hand down her leg. Surprisingly, she didn't stop me, so I took it a little further and moved up towards her kitty. She spread her legs a little and I rubbed her clit through the jeans she was wearing causing my shit to rock up hard as a brick.

"What I gotta do to make this right, Poe? I'm running out of ideas and I know you see a nigga really trying," I told her, and she locked her phone and sat it in the cupholder.

"Right now...I don't know, Meen. If you wasn't driving, I would tell you to close your eyes but since you can't, I just want you to imagine that I told you that I was pregnant, months and months and months go by. The baby comes and more time passes and then all of a sudden the real daddy comes up to you and tells you that your son is really his and has been named after him. Then you find out that while I was pregnant, we slept together a few times behind your back," Poe told me and I sighed.

"Man, I get it. I understand and I acknowledge how fucked up and childish my actions was. I hurt you and I know that. I promise you it'll never happen again. You got my word, Poe. I just wanna chance to show you my word is all I have that really means anything."

Poe sighed before looking out the window. She crossed her arms over her chest and sat back into her seat seeming like she was in deep thought. I really did get it all. Goat was out here now going through it after finding out that kids he had taken care of for years wasn't even his. The other night he came crying to me sick as a dog about it and I knew I would lose my shit if Poe ever told me Jr wasn't mine. I knew well enough that niggas could do dirt but couldn't take that shit that they dished out. I was already bowing out gracefully, because I knew I couldn't take it.

"Just want my baby back," I told Poe as I reached for her hand and pulled it to my lips. I kissed the back of it and forced her to interlock her fingers with mine.

For the remainder of the ride, we were quiet with me taking occasional glances at Poe. I would buy her the fucking world if I felt like it would get her to forgive me. A nigga was just lost out here. With a chick like Poe, her pops and even her bitch ass brother had showed her some boss shit, so nothing I did for her was nothing she wasn't already used to. Flowers, clothes, shoes, money, cars was shit she had seen already. I had to show her something different and I felt like I knew just what it was.

I bit down on my bottom lip before I brought Poe's hand up to my mouth and kissed it again. She glared at me and smiled slightly before taking her attention back outside the window.

"I love your ass," I told her, breaking the silence before I reached out and rubbed her leg.

"...I love you, too. Regardless of everything, I'm glad things worked out and you didn't go to jail. Jr. needs you, " Poe told me.

"What about you? You don't need me?"

"I'm trying not to," Poe's voice cracked and I sighed.

I didn't say shit else because I wasn't trying to make things worse than what they were. For now, I was gonna concentrate on the fact that a nigga was not going to jail. I had a big ass fucking party to throw. It was time for me to show off and stunt for the city. For the niggas that wished me to fail, I wanted all them muthafuckas to know I wasn't going nowhere.

Is you mad?
'Cause I'm gettin' cash (I'm gettin' cash)
It ain't my place (it ain't my place)
Bought a new Wraith (bought a new Wraith)

She in my face (she in my face)
I want her head (I want her head)

We had Magic City going up on a muthafucking Wednesday. This little ass club was packed to capacity and just like I had told Poe, the whole city was out—all that could fit anyway. I bobbed my head to **Lil Baby's** new track **Cash** while letting a handful of 20s go up in the air and drop down on all the butt naked strippers that were in my section.

I was gone off of Henny and weed, and I didn't give a fuck what Poe said, but tonight her ass was gon' give me some. All night her little ass had been acting real funny, walking around here with CoCo like that was her new buddy or something. She had on a little pair of shorts that showed her ass cheeks and this lil bra looking topping that had her new titties thanks to our son looking all delicious. Niggas was eye-fucking her heavy as hell, and I couldn't even stunt and make them even more mad cause she wasn't even giving me no damn play.

"Sup, Meen," some chick said in my ear, and I pulled back to look at her.

"Shit, sup ma'. Ain't seen you in a minute," I told Samantha, and she licked her lips while looking me over.

"Nigga cause you don't never answer my calls. I heard you and Kiani had a baby or whatever. That's still your boo?" she asked, and I frowned and shook my head.

Me and Samantha used to fuck with each other real heavy after my mama was killed. She was a cool ass chick from the East side that knew how to cook some fye ass dope according to the streets. A few times I thought about bringing her into my shit and teaching her to mix up the H just how I liked it, but I knew not to ever trust a hoe. One thing I could say about her was that she had some good box and was about her bread. Shawty stayed iced in some diamonds and rocking some designer shit.

"Why you look like that? Everybody know that's your girl or was your girl. Just was asking that's all, since you all of a sudden dropped me," Samantha smiled, and I took a sip of my drink.

"Everybody don't know me because if they did, they would know Kiani ain't been my girl in a minute," I told her, and out the corner of my eye I could see Poe and CoCo coming our way.

I looked in Poe's direction; the iced out Poetic chain she wore around her neck was glistening like a muthafucka under the club lights. I smirked when I saw the mug she was wearing only because she wanted to act like I wasn't shit to her, but the minute a broad got up in my face she was feeling a way. I held my hands up and stepped back letting her know I ain't want no smoke.

She rolled her eyes, before stepping in front of me with her back against me. I wrapped my arms around her waist and pulled her close to me. If I had known this was all this was gonna take, I would've had a bitch sent my way a long time ago. I didn't even send for Samantha, but damn, I was glad she came through.

"Bro...why the fuck is Jyelle here?" Goat said into my ear, and I looked around and spotted her not too far from us.

"Your ass ain't been home since you got them results, and I know she heard CoCo was around," I told him and when I saw Poe and Samantha having a conversation I frowned.

"Fuck is y'all talking about?" I asked, mugging Samantha, and she smiled deviously.

"She talks to Maino," Poe said while looking up at me.

"Oh yea?" was all I said as my head began to spin.

"Yep...I'mma tell him I saw y'all. We work together almost every day," Samantha yelled over the music and I didn't miss the way she winked at me before she walked off.

"What else she say?" I leaned over and asked Poe.

"She just asked me was I Maino's little sister cause I looked familiar and I told her yea. Then she started to telling me how they was messing around until she found out he had a girlfriend. Now they just business partners," Poe told me, and I nodded before I looked towards where Samantha had gone.

For the remainder of the night, we turned up while celebrating every stride that we had made. Not just in the game, but in life as well. A nigga had survived three bullets to the head and chest, beat a murder charge, and was now able to come home to my girl and my baby without worry. I could now freely move through the streets while expanding the empire that me and my family was building. Other than Moni still being on the loose, and the fact that I had to worry about the hit on Maino, shit was good. I was gonna handle both of them two and seeing how Samantha couldn't take her eyes off me let me know she was up to something. I didn't know which side she was on, but I was gonna find out before the night was up.

"Soooo...." Poe said while turning around towards me.

I sat down in the chair so that I could be face to face with her. She slid into my lap and I used both of my hands to grip her ass. Her lips was looking all juicy and shit, and I couldn't help but pull her lip into my mouth and then slide my tongue inside. We kissed for so long that I had forgot that we were in the club until I heard the DJ shouting out the Shakur Family over the mic.

"Sup..." I said to Poe.

"Was thinking about earlier and what you can do to fix it..." Poe led on and I raised my brow.

"I got some shit in the works, but tell me baby cause I'm down for whatever."

"I wanna meet with Kiani and I wanna know everything. I want to know the last time y'all slept together and what type of relationship y'all supposed to have. I want to hear it from her, and not you."

"Oh yea..." was all I said, before I shook my head.

"You got a problem with that?"

"Nah, baby. Whatever you wanna do. I'll text her right now and set it up," I told Poe and pulled out my phone.

Me: *Wanna set up something with you and Poe so y'all can meet and we can get everything understood.*

I showed Poe that I sent the message and before I could even do anything else, she took the phone out my hand and started going through my shit. I shook my head and grabbed my cup of Henny, tossing the rest of it back. The alcohol burned my throat and I stood to my feet so that I could let everybody know that I was about to call it a night.

"Why you leaving for?" Poe asked the moment we made it outside of the club.

"Gotta shoot out of town tomorrow, so I need to get up early."

"You didn't tell me you was going out of town."

"Probably cause you acting like you don't give a fuck about a nigga."

"How long are you supposed to be gone? Me and Jr. can't go?"

"Poe get in the car," I told her, and she frowned at me.

I opened Poe's door before walking around and hopping in the driver's side. Pulling out the lot, I turned onto the street and then looked over at Poe when I came to a stop at a red light. It was going on two in the morning and all the liquor and weed I had smoked had me in a daze. I reached over and rubbed Poe's bare thigh only for her to push my hand away.

"Mannnnn," I drawled. "Bet. Yo, I give up. Not doing this shit with you no more."

"I don't care, Ahmeen. It's just real funny you all of a sudden gotta go out of town," Poe spat as she crossed her arms over her chest.

"No all of a sudden nothing. I been having shit to do but the fuckin' trial was stopping me. Just cause I don't tell you about what goes on in my business, don't mean I don't have shit going on."

"Pretty sure you're going to see some bitch," Poe stupidly said, and I shook my head and chuckled.

"I should go see a bitch. Maybe I could get some pussy since your ass being funny," I spat, and Poe chuckled.

"Go right ahead. Just hurry up and get me home so I can go get my baby and leave. I'm done with your ass," Poe stated as she tapped her foot against the floor.

I sped through the streets trying to hurry up and get to the crib. I was over this shit for real. I was doing any and everything I had to fix the mistakes I had, but it was getting real old. Poe had me feeling like she wanted me to kiss her ass and I felt like I had done enough of that. Yea I fucked up, did a little lying, but besides that I knew for a fact that I treated her good. It was either she was gon' forgive me or she wasn't. I wasn't going out my way no more.

When I pulled into the driveway of the house, I got out and didn't even wait for Poe before going inside. I took the steps two at a time and went into the closet to find something to change into. I found a Gucci fit and quickly stripped out of what I was wearing and changed into that. I ain't know what I was about to do, but all that staying in the house and being a good nigga for a chick that wasn't tryna hear it was over. For the second time this year, I had gotten another chance at life. If Poe thought I was about to spend my time begging and pleading with her to move on so we could be happy then she had me fucked up. I was really realizing how quickly life could be snatched away from you within a heartbeat and I wasn't wasting no more time.

I grabbed the keys that I dropped onto the bed back up and then pulled my phone out of the pocket of my old jeans. Looking down at the phone, I saw that Kiani had text back from earlier. All she said was okay, but somehow, I knew it wasn't going to be that easy with her. She was never just an *okay* type of chick. It was always something with her, whether she popped off now or later.

Once I made it down the stairs and to the door so that I could leave, Poe was standing there with a deranged look on her face. I scratched my head before looking around and then back at her. I forgot she had told me about her crazy ass twin sister and wondered if she left off that she was mentally fucked up to.

"You must be about to take me to get Jr?" Poe asked as she leaned against the door picking at her nails.

"Nah...Pops said he keeping him until the morning. Move," I told her, and her head shot up.

"So, where you think you finna go?"

"Mannnnn," I drawled, and moved closer to her so that I could leave.

"Nigga, if you ain't going to pick up our son, then you ain't going nowhere. You can go back upstairs." Poe had the fuckin' audacity to say,e and I chuckled then ran my hand down my face. "I'm not laughing."

"Bro, you need to move. Why you wanna play with me right now?"

"I ain't playing with you...I don't wanna fight anymore. I miss you and I know that you're sorry. I forgive you, but if you leave, I'mma go crazy because I feel like you're going to leave me and be with somebody else," Poe admitted, and I pressed up against her, backing her against the door.

"Oh, you only forgive because you don't want me with anyone else?"

"No, I wanted to tell you that earlier, but got mad when you acted like you didn't want me meeting with Kiani."

"I told you I ain't care about you meeting with her. Me and that broad ain't got shit going on. She text back and said okay, so it's whatever."

"I miss you," Poe told me, and I bit down on my bottom lip while looking down at her.

"Miss you too."

I leaned over and picked Poe's little ass up from the floor and carried her up the stairs. She wrapped her arms around my neck while kissing all over my face and neck. My dick was already tented up in my jeans from the anticipation I had been feeling from not getting none since Poe cut me off. A nigga was already gone off weed and plenty Henny so I knew I was about to go in. I could barely even contain my excitement, and since she wanted to play with me, I was getting her ass pregnant on purpose.

"Shit!" Poe yelled when I tossed her onto the bed and ripped the shorts she had been wearing off. "So damn rough."

"Oh, you about to get fucked," I told her, and she giggled. "I ain't playing with you."

I climbed out of my clothes and onto the bed. Pushing Poe towards the middle of it, I waited until she had slid her pants off before I was going inside of her. My eyes shut as the warmth from her pussy caused my dick to grow even harder. My shit thumped while inside of her and I bit down on my lip before I propped one leg over my arm and started pounding inside of her.

"Damn it!"

"Baby..." I grunted, before I popped her titties out of the bralette.

I sucked her right nipple into my mouth and then flickered my tongue back and forth. Poe's pussy tightened around my dick and even the liquid courage couldn't stop my shit from feeling like it was ready to nut.

I grabbed Poe's face and forced her to look at me. Pulling her bottom lip into my mouth, I stroked in and out of her, going as deep as I could. She wrapped both of arms around me and then her legs. Her lips locked with mine and I felt her starting to shake underneath me.

"Mmmmmgh...I'm about to come, Meen. Babbbbbyyyy!" she crooned, her pussy tightening just before her cum dripped all over me.

I rolled her onto her stomach, propping her ass up in the air before sliding in from behind. Spreading her cheeks, I slid my thumb into her butt while my dick went in and out her soaking pussy.

"Shit, Meen! You gonna make me come again," Poe cried, and when she lost the arch in her back, I smacked her on the ass.

"Get back right," I told, pulling at her stomach so that she was in perfect position.

Instead of putting my thumb back, I used my saliva, getting two of my fingers nice and wet before I slid them both in her ass. Her pussy became wetter and I shook my head knowing that I was about to nut. My fingers went in and out of her at the same rate as my dick did. Poe suddenly started backing it up like crazy and before I knew it, she was screaming and squirting at the same time.

"Oh, my Godddddddddd!"

"Got damn girl," I told her, before I bust the biggest nut of my life inside of her.

My heart was beating fast as shit and I rolled over onto the bed and just laid there. I felt like I had three different type of highs going all at once. One from the weed, one from the nut and one from the shit that Poe had whispered into my ear.

"Is it too late to say that yes I will marry you."

17

GOAT

It was going on four in the morning and my ass was drunk as a skunk. I had thrown probably a hundred bands at some hoes tonight and wasn't even sweating it. My brother was a free man, and even though Chanel had to die for it to happen, the shit had to be done. I didn't even tell Latrel or Ahmeen what had taken place with shawty. Shit when Ahmeen came to me saying that it was being said that Moni had killed Chanel, I just let that shit rock. I felt bad enough and didn't want to put more onto my little brother than what he had already been dealing with.

"Thank you for walking me to the door," CoCo slurred, and I frowned at her.

"Fuck is you talking about walking you to the door? I'm coming inside. A nigga hungry and I know you can still cook even though you drunk," I told her before I smacked her ass.

She giggled before taking out her keys and unlocking the door. We both stumbled inside and I shut the door behind me but didn't lock it since I was going to be leaving back out soon. I followed CoCo into the kitchen and watched as she took out two pots and placed them on the stove.

"Lucky for your greedy ass there's Chicken and Dumplings left-over from earlier. My grandmother actually made this and it's soooo good," CoCo said while closing her eyes as if she could savor the taste.

"Damn grandma here," I said and took my jacket off. I rubbed my hands together before going to find me a plate. "Hell yea. Grandma cooks better than you, so I definitely want some."

"Oh, fuck you," CoCo mushed me, and I chuckled.

"Shitttt, don't act like you don't know," I told her with a shrug.

I fixed me a big ass plate of Chicken and Dumplings along with some of the homemade biscuits. After heating everything up, I grabbed a seat at the table and tore into my food. I was all into it that I hadn't even realized that CoCo had been staring at me.

"Sup..." I asked her, and she smiled.

"So, what's up with you and Jy? You invite me out to the club and when she shows, you stayed near me? Y'all done?"

"Hell yea, I'm done. Not gonna act like I ain't did my own dirt, but this shit foul as fuck. Really let me think for six years them kids was mine. I don't even know if I should even tell my boys are not or just don't even say shit."

"Well, we were all young back then. I'm sure she probably just didn't know how to tell you."

"Nahhhh, fuck that. She knew she fucked somebody else raw. Shit she should've told me."

"You never came and told her when you was over here fuckin' me raw... at least not until I ended up pregnant," CoCo argued and I shook my head.

"Different situation man. Shit you taking up so much for her, do I need to be getting Giaria and Gem tested?"

"Boy don't ever insult me," CoCo said with a roll of her eyes before she took the empty plate from in front of me.

I got up and stepped in behind her and wrapped my arms around her waist. Burying my face into her neck, I placed kisses on her skin, feeling the chill bumps that suddenly popped up.

"Stop...Goat, I ain't dumb for you like I used to be. You can't run over here no more when you and Jy got problems and think I'mma just open up my legs for you anymore. That ship has sailed and I done grew up, if you can't tell."

"I know, and I can tell. I ain't here cause we having problems. I'm here cause I wanna be and because I'm done with Jy for real this time. And don't act like you don't know how I feel about you," I told her and kissed her ear.

"Right...I know, you showed me when you chose Jyelle and went and had two more kids with her, regardless if they're yours or not. Damn it, Goat, get off of me."

I backed away from CoCo and went and sat back on my seat. CoCo wet a rag and came over to wash the table off. When she got to the spot where I was sitting, I grabbed her hand and looked up at her. Her golden-brown skin looked like it was glistening underneath the lights above us.

"I'm about to go wake your kids up. Let me go," CoCo urged and pursed her lips together.

"I can't have none?" I asked her, my eyes veering to the triangle that sat between her legs.

"Noooo, no, you cannot. Why you wanna play with me for?"

"I'm not playing with you. You know how hard it be for me not to fuck with you?"

I stood to my feet and wrapped my arms around her again. She turned her head to the side to keep from looking at me and I started kissing all over her neck. Both of her hands landed on my chest to push me away, but I only pulled her closer before my touch landed on her ass.

"I'm not about to keep being your side chick, nigga. I deserve better than what you be trying to give me, and you know that. I know I'm not skinny and built anything like Jyelle, but I do know that somebody wants me and will treat me right."

"That's what you think? I chose Jy because she's smaller than you?"

"That's what you niggas always do. Love picking the foreign looking chicks with the nice body just to end up with a hoe. Niggas will leave a good wholesome woman that will love you down to your dirty draws and never do you no wrong for a bitch that will fuck your brother," CoCo said, and I pushed her away and looked at her.

"Hell you mean, fuck my brother? So you saying, Jy fucked my brother?" I asked her, crossing my arms over my chest.

"What difference does it make, Goat? You gon' leave her alone, for real? It's not like she ain't did shit before and you stayed with her." CoCo frowned.

"Man tell me what the hell you know and stop playing with me. You wanna keep dropping these hints and shit like that's cool or something. What brother she fucked and who told you that shit?"

"Word is, Jy fucked Moni and y'alls last kid and the one she miscarried was his, too. That was told to me by a former associate of mine whom was told by Jy's ex-bestie Ashlon. Apparently, they fell out about something and Ashlon is going around telling all of Jy's secrets," CoCo said and I grimaced.

I knew it had to be some truth to it, because Jy did have a best friend by the name of Ashlon and they did fall out a few months ago. Ashlon was mad because I wouldn't fuck her and when I told Jy what kinda shit she was on, they had a big ass fight. I guess Ash was feeling some type of way.

"Damn, so Moni really out here on some more shit. Nigga just don't give a fuck," I said and sucked my teeth.

"Yea...I been wanting to tell you but shit was crazy enough and I really wasn't sure if you was gonna believe me or even care."

"You ain't never lied to me. I'm mad as fuck you ain't tell me the shit when you first found out, but I appreciate you for looking out. A nigga could've spent the next 10-15 years looking dumb."

"Right...how you had me looking."

I shook my head and sighed before I rushed CoCo and wrapped my arms around her. I started kissing all over her, not even giving her a chance to tell me no. Once we was inside of her room, I closed and locked the door behind me. I removed CoCo's dress and when I saw that she wasn't wearing any panties, I bit down on my lip before sliding down between her legs.

Burying my face between her box, I licked around the folds of her pussy before sucking her clit into my mouth. She immediately started to gush and I slid a finger inside and started to press against her G-Spot.

"Oh, my God, Ge'Loni," CoCo moaned while rotating her hips.

I flickered my tongue over her button causing her legs to tremble like a leaf. She grabbed my head, shoving me deeper into her cave and I attacked her pussy with my tongue. After pressing against her spot, and playing with her clit, CoCo's juices squirted out of her landing right on my face. I slurped every part of her up, before standing to my feet and stepping out of my jeans.

"Wow...you can't be doing this to me, Goat," CoCo protested and tried to close her legs, but I pushed them right back open.

I slid inside of her and started working my dick in and out of her slippery box. Her shit was tight as fuck and swallowed me up like a glove. She was trying to close her legs, but I pushed her shit all the way open, trying to go as deep as I can.

"Fuckkkk!" CoCo moaned.

"You trying to wake them kids up?" I asked her. "Or even worse, grandma?"

"Stop going so deep nigga. Pull back."

"Hell nah, this pussy so good I'm trying to feel all of it. With your stingy ass."

"You made me break my celibacy. Seven, long hard months," CoCo cried, and I leaned over and pulled her right breast into my mouth.

I circled her nipples and decided that I was going to make love to her rather than just fucking her. Knowing that I had been the last one inside of her made me want to cherish her a little bit more. I took my time, going slower and giving more meaningful strokes. Every now and then, I would pull out and start back licking her pussy and causing her to go crazy.

Before I knew it, CoCo and I had gone for over two hours before I finally allowed myself to nut. When it was over, we sat in the bed talking until her ass fell asleep on me. I got up and went to wash my dick off before sliding my pants back on. All that fucking had caused me to work up another appetite, so I went inside of the kitchen to heat me up another plate.

I don't know what it was, but something felt real off. I felt like someone was standing behind me, and when I turned around, I expected to see one my kids, but instead saw Moni. I quickly reached for a knife just as he fired a shot at me, luckily missing. I charged at him, knocking his ass to the ground and bringing my fist up to punch him in the face.

"Bitch ass nigga!" I yelled and tried to hit him again, when I felt him shove the gun in my side.

I grabbed at his right wrist that held onto the gun and used all of the strength that I could to try to knock it away from him. He was able to fire another shot, which this time grazed against my back. I grimaced when it felt like someone had pressed a burning piece of coal into my shit.

"Oh no! Gemini! Oh, God, Gem!" I heard CoCo crying and when I looked up and saw that my son was laying on the floor covered in blood, I lost it. "Maw-Maw!"

"Oh shit..." Moni said while looking at Gemini too.

I used that moment to get the gun away from him. I climbed to my feet and kicked him in the side, and then brought my foot up to kick him again. His body jerked and caused the gun to fall out of his hand. He tried to reach for it, but I kicked him in the face and leaned over and grabbed it. I raised it and pointed it to his head.

"Moni no! The kids!" CoCo yelled, and I snarled. "Nooo!"

"Aye, nigga you better get the fuck up outta here," I told Moni, hating that I had to let this dude make it.

I kept the gun pointed at him and he climbed to his feet. He turned to look at me, tears falling from his eyes as he stared at me for a good while. I shook my head, feeling real fucked up that shit had come down to this. We was supposed to be family...brothers, and taking over the world right now, but somehow it had come to this nigga wanting to take us all out.

"No matter what, I would've never done to your girl or kids what you done to Chanel. You gon' see me again, Ge'Loni. I got you nigga,"

Moni grimaced before he turned around and ran out of the front door.

I rushed to make sure he was gone, before I then went to check on my son. He was laying in his mother's arms with a scared look on his face. His hazel eyes looked up at me and he gripped at his side before reaching out for my hand. I kneeled down beside him, before placing a kiss on his forehead.

"You gon' be alright, Gem. Just hang in there," I told him, and he smiled.

"It don't even hurt. But daddy, you should've killed him," Gemini said and I sighed, knowing good and damn well he was right.

18

AHMEEN

A Few Days Later...

"S up..." I said to Kiani as she walked up to the table that Poe and I were sitting at.

We were sitting outside in the balcony dining area at the Cheesecake Factory. Poe and I had been at the hospital for the last couple of days with Goat and my nephew Gemini. I didn't even make it out of town and had put my shipment on hold until I handled all my problems first. Last thing I wanted was for that fuck nigga to get to my girl and baby while I was away. Security or not, only nigga I trusted was Latrel and that nigga wasn't that good that he could do everything by himself.

I stood up and grabbed Kiani's baby from her and sat down with him sitting in my lap. Slob dribbled down the sides of his mouth as he sucked on the bib that was wrapped around his neck. It seemed like he'd gotten a lot bigger since the last time I had seen him in the courtroom. She had been hitting me up ever since then, but I had been ignoring her, besides when I told her that I wanted her and my girl to talk.

"Aye, look, I really wanted to sit y'all down so that you can let it be known that me and you ain't got nothing going on. Yea we fucked a few times but that was way before the baby and before me and Poe really even got serious. Every time you hit me up on some dumb shit about us being together, I always tell you I got a girl," I said and Kiani's bottom lip began to tremble.

"Wow...you could've just told me this over the phone or through text message. You really brought me out here to embarrass me in front of your *girl*," Kiani snarled and I shrugged.

"Bro, look, ain't nobody tryna embarrass nobody. My girl...well my fiancé was feeling some kinda way and I'm tryna fix it and show her that me and you ain't got nothing going on. I fucked up by sleeping with you back when you was pregnant, but the shit never happened again after that."

"Bro...so it's bro now," Kiani chuckled. "No baby, or love, or bae...bro, huh?"

"You heard what the fuck I said. Why you playing games with me right now? You know I can walk the fuck away right now and never look back. Stop acting like you don't know me. I'm trying to do this shit like a fuckin' man, let you meet my fuckin' wife, so you know who your kid gon be around and you wanna act like I be bothering you and tryna fuck or some'. Stop with the bullshit.

You chose to get high and I chose to move the fuck on. I'm happy and I'm good and I ain't gon keep pretending I wanna have something with you cause I don't want you out here getting high, but we all grown as fuck. If you can't do it for this little boy then shit, that's your problem not mine. I'm good on you shawty, and I'm saying that for you in front of her, so you can't make it like I'm fronting on nobody," I said, grimacing at how bad Poe's leg was shaking against mine. I knew that meant she was upset.

"You're happy now, Poe?" Kiani asked as tears slid down her face. She looked at Poe and pursed her lips together. "Seeing another woman hurt brings you pleasure?"

"Man, shut the fuck up," I snapped and sucked my teeth.

"I don't want my baby around her. Since she's so adamant about hurting me, there's no telling what she will try and do to my child," Kiani had the nerve to say, and I shook my head.

"Alright... I'mma go to the car," Poe told me and stood up.

"You're happy about taking a man from out his relationship huh? I'm pretty sure you were happy to see me get shot that day. Probably made you feel real good that I was possibly gon' die so that you can have Ahmeen all to yourself. Talking about fiancé! Nigga I'm the one that was with your ass before all this! Then this bitch comes along and you allow her to give her child our son's name!"

"Nah bitch, I gave my son my name! Fuck is you talking about."

"Bitch? You really gon' call me a bitch in front of our son? But I guess it's fuck our baby, right? You know what? You got it, Ahmeen. You and Little Ms. Poetic can kiss me and my child's ass. How about you won't be seeing him ever again," Kiani said before she shot up to her feet.

She grabbed little man from my arms and stormed off in the same direction that she had come from. I knew the shit wasn't going to go well, but this was what Poe wanted. If it made her feel better then that was all that mattered. I had been guarding Kiani's feelings for a good while now, trying be as supportive and helpful as I could be with her, but fuck all that babysitting shit now. She was a grown ass woman and if she wanted to get back out there and fuck for a drop knowing she had a kid then that was on her. My priorities were Poe and the kid we had together. I had fucked up enough to know better at this point. I was sorry for hurting Kiani, but I refused to ever let my baby be the one catching the heat ever again.

"Soooo, that went well," Poe said, and I chuckled.

"Mannnnn," I drawled. "Childish as fuck. Told you she be tryna handle me and shit. She always wanna play victim and use her damn addiction against me and my dumb ass let her. I should've never let her come at me like that to begin with."

"Yea, well hopefully she'll come around and stop acting stupid. I don't want to be the cause of you losing time with your son."

"I'm good with our kid and that's on everything."

"Don't be like that, Meen. Don't say that. That's your child too regardless of who his mother is."

"Yea, whatever," I said and waved her off.

I bit down on my lip and then leaned over and kissed hers. She sucked my tongue into her mouth then pulled back before she started giggling. I grabbed her left hand and stared down at the new rock I had picked up yesterday. I had dropped a hundred thousand out this pretty muthafucka too. Money wasn't shit to me. I wasn't going to lie though and act like after Poe went to sleep the night she told me that she was gon' accept my proposal, that my drunk ass wasn't out in the field looking for the one I threw. I had the whole goon squad outside with flash lights for hours combing every inch, but I knew one of them bitch ass niggas had my shit and was probably waiting on the right time to quit.

"Babe, iced the fuck out," I said acting as if she was blinding me. "Just wait til your new lil piece come."

"What new piece?" Poe asked with her brow raised. She took a sip of her soda and then looked back at me.

"That shit says Meen's Girl, in yellow and black diamonds. Got a little black heart next to her."

Poe burst into laughter. "Nigga, ain't nobody wearing no chain that says Meen's Girl."

"Shitttttttt, Jr. got your ass looking thick and shit. Need everybody to know you mine. As a matter of fact, let me make a post on all my social media accounts right now. I'mma tag you and put WCW. Hold the fuck up," I told her then pulled out my phone.

"Boy today is Friday."

"Shit...I'll just put Wife then. Fuck is you saying. I ain't posted on social media in about a year. Niggas gon' know it's real today. Let me make some folks mad."

"You are so silly. Give me a kiss..." Poe said, and I kissed her lips.

She leaned over to where I was, and then licked the side of my face. I frowned, but it was weird shit like that, that had a nigga in deep with her. I never even believed in soulmates until I had run into

Poe. After all the bullshit cleared, and we had a chance to really be at peace, I knew our shit was going to be more than dope.

ERRCHHHHHHH! BAMM!

"What the fuck?" I said shooting to my feet.

I looked out into the parking lot from where we had been sitting in and noticed that a car had ran into a light pole. It took me a few seconds to realize that it was Kiani's Audi. My eyes bucked, and I pushed the table back and took off running out of the restaurant. The front of the car and quickly engulfed in flames and I ran harder and faster trying to get to them.

"I can't believe she did that! It was like it was on purpose," I heard someone say as I tried to pull the back door open.

"Fuck! Kiani, unlock the door!" I yelled and tugged at the handle again.

Seeing the flames getting bigger, I drew back and punched my fist through the back window, causing the glass that shattered to cut my entire hand up. I gritted as I unlocked the door, pulled it open, and quickly unbuckled little man's car seat. Snatching him out of the car, I rushed him over to the sidewalk and sat him down.

"Oh, my God, it was a baby in there! Someone call for help," I heard someone yell out.

"Get him, Poe!" I yelled noticing that she was standing nearby, frozen in place.

I turned back to go after Kiani, but the moment I heard the engine making cracking and a loud popping noise, I knew that it was too late. I peddled backwards, causing others that were close by to do so as well. The hood flew back as flames exploded into the air damn near burning the entire front half of the car within seconds. At that point, I knew that Kiani was dead.

A couple of hours later, me, Poe, my pops, Goat and Kiani's parents, Quentin and Teresa, were sitting in the waiting area. Once the ambulance and firetruck arrived on the scene, they rushed Kiani's baby to the hospital and even had done the same for her. She was already dead. I knew it was no way she could've survived that explosion, but I didn't say anything to Quentin and Teresa about it. Kiani was their only child and I knew that it would fuck them up knowing that they had lost her. I didn't even know how to explain it to them, so I only told them that I didn't know what was going on.

"Excuse me, Mr. and Mrs. Taylor?"

"Yes," Quentin jumped to his feet with Teresa and my pops joining him. I buried my head into my hands already knowing how this shit was about to go. "Are they okay?"

"Kiani, she was badly burned in the fire. When she arrived, we tried to do everything we could but it was just too..."

"Oh, my God! Don't tell me that! Don't tell me that!" Teresa cried, and Quentin wrapped his arms around her.

"I'm so sorry for your loss, Mr. and Mrs. Taylor. We are currently working on the baby. It's possible that he might need some blood. Do you have the information for the child's father?" the doctor asked, and Quentin turned to me.

"Yea...he's right there..." Quentin said, and I stood up.

"Yes...like I was saying to your son's grandparents. The baby will need blood. Normally the father or mother will match, but since Kiani has..."

"I'm not his father," I said, and everyone looked at me.

"What the fuck is you talking about?" Quentin barked, getting up in my face.

I sucked my teeth and stepped back a couple of feet. I understood that Quentin was upset, but I wouldn't hesitate to knock his ass out if I had to. Kiani's child wasn't mine. Soon as I had gotten out of the hospital and was well enough to go and see Kiani and the baby, I had Goat go and get a home DNA kit for me. We did the test and sent it off, the next week, I found out that her child wasn't mine, but I never said anything.

Every time I came around, all Quentin, Kiani, and Teresa talked about was how detrimental I was to her sobriety. They made it seem like I was the key to her staying sober, so I told myself that I would do what I needed to do to help keep her clean. I played nice and I told myself that I would be there for her kid because deep down I knew she probably didn't even know who the fuck the father was. That was the only reason I really didn't care to tell Poe about Kiani or the baby. To me, after I had found out the results, it wasn't shit to tell. That was the only reason why I named my son Ahmeen. The child I had with Poe was my true heir, and I wasn't being funny about it or lying when I had told Poe that. It was the truth and it meant more to me than she knew for my son, my flesh and blood to carry my name.

"I took a DNA test and the baby ain't mine. I was trying to be the bigger person and step in and be a father figure for the kid, but I didn't think none of this was going to happen," I said to Quentin, and his jaws contorted as defeat seemed to settle in.

"Man...shit I can't believe this," Quentin said before he broke down.

"I'll give blood. I don't know if it's going to do any good, but I will try," I told him, and he nodded before he fell into the seat.

"Babe, I'm going to go to the restroom," Poe told me, and I looked over at her and nodded.

"Come right back," I told her when she walked off.

"Why didn't you tell anybody?" my Pops asked me, and I shrugged.

"I don't know. Shit, y'all kept treating me like I was the reason Kiani got on that shit in the first place. I already knew if she found that shit out, she was gon probably use it as a reason to get back out there, so I ain't say nothing. Y'all wasn't going do shit but blame me for that, too."

"Ok, let's just get everyone tested, and let's go for that. Worst case is that we will just have to get some from the blood bank," the doctor told us, and I nodded. "I will get someone from the lab to come and get everyone shortly."

I sat back down in my seat and purposely buried my head in my phone so that no one would say shit to me. I hated what happened to Kiani and I hated that little man was even having problems, but I wasn't about to let them make me feel bad about the choices that their daughter had made. Majority of the people that were out there and had witnessed the crash said that Kiani had done it on purpose. She obviously was trying to kill herself and her son, which was real fucked up on her part.

Wife: *I can't believe you lied about that too Meen. Really.*

I shook my head and sighed before I replied to Poe's text.

Me: *That's really why I wasn't trying to tell you, but truthfully, when did you ever hear me refer to her baby by the name she gave him. Eventually I was gon tell you and her the truth, but I was trying to wait until I knew she was good. It was dumb of me but don't sit here and be mad at me for stepping up and being a father figure for that little boy.*

I waited for Poe to text me back, and when she didn't, I got up and looked for the restroom. I swear if she started tripping on me again, I was gon' flip the fuck out. I wasn't about to deal with this back and forth shit. Poe was either in this or she wasn't.

Once I found the restrooms, I tapped on the women's door before I pushed it open and stuck my head inside. I looked around, trying to see if I could tell if she was in one of the stalls. She had been gone long enough for her to have handled her business and been done by now.

I went to my call log in my phone and pressed down on her name. The line only rung twice before I was forwarded to the voicemail. I sucked my teeth and then tried again only for her to forward my call again.

Me: *Yo why the fuck you wanna play with me. Where the hell you at?*

I leaned against the wall near the restrooms waiting for Poe to text me back. After it seemed like she wasn't going to, I stormed in the restroom and checked every stall. My heart dropped thinking that she'd run away from me again. I rushed out of the restroom and tried calling her again. When it had gone to voicemail again, I panicked and took off running, looking for the other restrooms.

"Man, I swear to God, Poe."

I went to every restroom on the floor before and when I didn't find her, I went back to where everyone was still waiting in the waiting room. I was hoping she had found her way back there and was just being stubborn, but I didn't see her anywhere.

"Bro, Pops, y'all seen Poe?" I asked them and they both hopped to their feet.

"Nah, I thought she said she was going to the bathroom," Goat said and I shook my head then walked off.

He followed behind me as I headed towards the exit of the hospital's Emergency room. I went to the contact information between me and Poe, and then waited for the map under her name to pull up her location. Ever since the last time she ran off, and then Javier coming to me saying they had put a hit out on her, I made sure she always shared her location with me in case I ever needed to find her.

After a few seconds, a circle that had her initials popped up and started moving across the screen. My jaws clenched as I rushed to my car with Goat following behind me. I pulled my keys from my pocket and unarmed the alarm right as we made it to the car.

"Where y'all going?" Pop yelled after us.

"She left! I'mma be right back!"

"How the fuck she leave?" Goat asked as we got inside of the car.

"I don't know, but I swear to God, she gon' make me really fuck her up. She really trying a nigga's patience for real," I said as I skated out of the parking lot while following wherever the circle took me.

19

POETIC

"Where you taking me?" I cried out, as De'Moni snatched me out the back seat of his car and started to drag me by my hair.

I swung at him and tried to get away, but he turned around and slapped me across my face. The taste of blood filled my mouth while salty tears started to run down my cheeks. I didn't even notice where De'Moni had come from earlier, but the moment I had stepped foot out of the women's restroom at the hospital, he was standing right there. He pressed a gun into my stomach, snatched my phone away, and told me that if I screamed, he was going to shoot me, so I didn't.

It was when I saw him that I realized why Ahmeen was so over-protective of me and wished that I had never left his side. Now, I wasn't even sure if I was going to ever see him or our son again. The thought of it caused my entire body to tremble and me to feel weak at the knees.

"Bring your ass the fuck on!" De'Moni yelled and snatched a handful of my hair.

He pushed me forward and I cautiously looked around trying to see if I can determine where we were. It was dark, and the area didn't look familiar to me at all. I knew that we were in the hood though just based off all the worn down houses and older model cars that were around.

De'Moni walked up to the door of the home we were in front of, then used his shoulder to pop it open. He then jerked me inside and pushed me so hard that I fell to the ground. The home was pitch black inside and I couldn't see anything or what was around me.

"Please, just let me go," I cried, tapping my hands against the floor as I tried to feel my way around.

"Shut the fuck up, bitch," De'Moni told me and I sat up and wrapped my hands around my knees. "Your ass ain't so muthafuckin' tough how you was when you was accusing me of killing your sister."

"It wasn't me. It was my sister and I was just hurt at the time. Now I know that you didn't do it and I'm sorry for blaming you. Please just let me go," I pleaded with him.

"Nah, I'mma put your ass on Facebook live, torture you how they did my girl, and then murk your ass for the world to see. You ain't have no issues with embarrassing me in front of a bunch of mutha-fuckas so don't have no issues now. Keep that same energy ma," De'Moni told me and finally some lights came on.

I blinked my eyes before looking around the home. It looked so familiar, but I couldn't recall right off hand where I had seen this place before. The furniture was old and dusty, and the walls contained a good amount of dirt and spider webs, but I swore I had either been here before or had seen this place in my dreams.

"Pick your head up hoe," De'Moni told me before sitting on the coffee table and staring down at me.

His eyes were red and low and looked like he had even more tats on his face since the last time I saw him in the courtroom snitching his soul away. The nigga looked deranged and as if he should have been locked up in the same asylum as my sister Lyric.

"Facebook, everybody say what's up to little Ms. Poetic King. Bitch think she's a princess but she ain't nothing but a hood hoe just like her sister Lyric. This is Ahmeen's little bitch and y'all about to watch this hoe suck my dick, before I put a bullet in her forehead. Ge'Loni, my fuckin brother killed my girl and I know that Ahmeen had to be the one to order the hit. Ge'Loni is his little bitch and I know he wouldn't have done it without his say. So, if anybody wanna know, just know that De'Moni didn't snap for nothing," De'Moni said while pointing his phone right at me.

I held my head down forcing De'Moni to reach out and kick my leg. My mouth dropped open as a cry escaped my lips. I looked up at him while tears glided down my face. I knew that this nigga was for real and that he was really going to kill me. Of all the things that I thought would happen to me in this lifetime, I never thought this would be my fate.

Maino and my daddy used to tell me, Lyric, and Melody all the time about stuff like this, but I never thought it would ever come true. I tried to calm my soul and think positive. Think about the fact that I would finally be able to see my baby girl again. I missed Melody so much and only because I knew I had someone to be with when I left this earth was the only reason I forced myself to stop crying.

I took in a deep breath and when De'Moni came closer to me and towered over me like a dark shadow, I looked up at him and shrugged my shoulders. I wouldn't even give him the satisfaction of seeing me sweat anymore.

"Do what you gotta do nigga," I told him, and he chuckled.

"Ohhhhhh, there go that tough talk. Bitch, yo.."

POW!

My body shook, and I jumped back as droplets of blood fell down onto my face. I quickly peddled backwards just as De'Moni's body fell forward onto the wooden floor. My eyes bucked wide as my heart fell into the pit of my stomach. I almost pissed myself, but when I looked up to see Ahmeen and Goat, I calmed down and started crying tears of joy.

Ahmeen rushed towards me and snatched me up from the floor. I wrapped my arms around him and started kissing all over his face. I couldn't believe he had found me, but quickly remembered him forcing me to share my location with him. I remembered thinking how petty he was being and that it was just another way for him to show how much control he had over me. Once again he had proven to me that it wasn't about control or pettiness at all and that he was really just doing what needed to be done to look out for me.

"Oh, my God. I thought he was going to kill me. Oh my God," I cried, holding onto Ahmeen for dear life.

"Mannnnnn," Ahmeen drawled. "I don't know what the fuck just happened, but I wasn't expecting this."

"Wait...he was on live," I told Ahmeen, remembering that De'Moni had started a live video.

"What?" he questioned.

"He was on live. He was recording us."

Goat rushed over to where De'Moni's body was. He rolled him over and found his phone underneath him. Looking down at it, he then ended the live video before dropping the phone on top of Moni's chest.

"Let's go," Meen told him, turning to leave out of the house.

"The inside of the house looks so familiar," I told Ahmeen.

"That's my grandma's old house. You probably remember it from all my pictures," Meen said, and that was when it came to me.

Meen placed me in the backseat of the Bentley and got inside next to me while Goat got in the driver's seat. He quickly pulled away from the house, and I snuggled up under Ahmeen and rested my head into his chest.

"I don't wanna live here anymore...in Atlanta. This place holds too many bad memories for me. Can we please leave? Please, Ahmeen?" I looked up at him, and he placed a soft kiss on my forehead.

"Whatever you want baby," he told me, and I settled my head back into his chest.

"Promise me we'll leave soon," I begged, only this time he didn't say anything and only rubbed my back.

I knew this was Ahmeen's home and where he made his money,

but after everything that happened, a fresh start felt like the best thing for me. I wanted to raise my son where nobody knew my name, and where nobody cared about the fact that I was Poetic King. I wanted to feel safe and feel like I didn't have to always watch over my back. I just wanted to go.

20
GOAT

3 months later…

"Oh, my God, this is so dope. Look at the mountains, Goat," CoCo gleamed like a big ass kid as she leaned over the railing of the boat.

"A'ight girl, you better be careful before you fall the fuck over," I told her while looking around.

I couldn't believe I let these muthafuckas talk me into taking a boat into the middle of the Pacific Ocean so we could go scuba diving. This was not some shit that niggas did, but somehow CoCo convinced Poe, and she had Ahmeen thinking it was a good idea. That nigga was so pussy whipped though that Poe could convince him out that recipe that the nigga still refused to give up.

We were vacationing in Hawaii and had been here already for a couple of days. I wasn't gonna lie and say that the shit wasn't beautiful because it was. The water was a color blue that I had never seen before and in some parts, you could look down and see towards the bottom. We had already spotted a few Dolphins and turtles and although I was a bit intrigued, a nigga was a bit nervous. Looking around, it looked like we were in the middle of nowhere and far as fuck if something was to happen and we had to swim.

"Looooook! Look at that!" Poe screamed, her excitement causing both me and Ahmeen to laugh.

Over the last few months, all these muthafuckas did was vacation. Ahmeen refused to move away from Atlanta and had promised Poe that he would take her somewhere new every month if she let the idea of moving go. So far, they had been to Vegas, Punta Cana, Jamaica, and now here to Hawaii. This last time, I had opted to join them and so did my pops and his new lady Asia that he'd been seeing.

CoCo and I were taking things a day at a time. It took all the bullshit and us almost losing our son Gemini for me to realize that I never should've left her to begin with. Unfortunately, I had fucked up her trust and she was skeptical about letting me all the way in. Either way though, things had been good between us. I was sure to do all the things for her that I had never took the time out to do before.

We went out on dates weekly, and then out as a family every week as well. I chose not to tell the boys that I thought were mine that I wasn't their biological father because I was all they knew. I loved them just the same and would always treat them as if they were mine. Me and Jyelle didn't speak at all unless it concerned the kids and I had never even asked her about whether or not the kids possibly belonged to Moni. I didn't even care to know. The nigga was dead and it wasn't like if he was alive that I would ever allow them around him.

"You ready, my boy. Tighten up," Ahmeen said as he smacked me on the back and handed me a scuba diving vest.

"Bruh, I don't know about this. That water big as fuck," I told him and motioned my hand towards the ocean.

"Bruh, if you let CoCo and Poe get in and you don't, I'm clowning you for the rest of your life. You'll forever be pussy to me."

"I'll just be a pussy then. I'mma let y'all have that," I told them, and they all shook their heads at me.

"Goat come on! Don't be no damn bitch," CoCo told me, and I

sighed. "Just get in and if you don't like it then you can get back on the boat."

I shook my head and put all the equipment on while listening to the instructor tell us what and what not to do. My heart was beating fast as hell, but I sucked it up and decided to just experience this shit. Hell, I had done been shot at multiple times, in a couple of car accidents, plus some other shit, so drowning or being ate by a shark probably wasn't as bad as it sounded. If I had survived that, I was sure that I could survive this.

Once I had gotten into the water, it actually wasn't as bad as I thought. CoCo had convinced me to go under so that the crew could take a picture of us. A nigga was low-key freaked out and a little but excited at the same time. All kinds of colorful fish and turtles were swimming around like it was normal. I had never seen nothing like that in my life and started to get curious. I relaxed and enjoyed the scenery so much that I had forgotten that we were in the middle of nowhere in the ocean.

After staying out in the water for a good thirty minutes, we all got back onto the boat and headed back to the facility we left from. From there they took us back to our hotel where we were staying at the Outriggers Reef in Waikiki.

"I had so much fun today and I'm glad you got in the water," CoCo told me, and I looked at her and nodded.

"Yea, that shit was straight. I ain't gon' lie," I told her, and she chuckled.

"Sooooo, I have something to tell you, and I don't know how you're going to take it," CoCo said just as we were walking back into our room.

"What's up?"

"My period was late, and I ummmm took a pregnancy test before we came here and it was positive. I wasn't sure how to tell you because I had been thinking about getting an abortion. I know you got a lot on your plate right now and..."

"Why the hell would you get an abortion? Shit, I'm a grown man. I know what happens when you have unprotected sex. If I wasn't ready for the responsibility, then I would've at least made sure to strap up?" I said and walked over to her.

"So...you want me to keep it?"

"You kill it then we gon' have a problem." I told her, and she chuckled, happily.

"Okay...wow," CoCo said.

"Come here," I told her and climbed out of the swim shorts I was wearing. I grabbed her hand and laid back onto the bed with my dick pointing right at the ceiling.

Coco removed her swimming suit and climbed onto the bed, sliding her opening down onto my shaft. I groaned before reaching out to grab a handful of her breasts.

"Damn, I ever told you I loved you?" I asked, causing her to blush as she slid up and down my dick.

"Not as much as I would like to hear," CoCo said, her eyes squinting as she rode me good and slow. "But I love you, Goat. Please don't ever play with me again. I'm so scared that all this is going to come to an end and I'm going to lose you again," CoCo confessed as she eased up and down on my dick.

I squinted my eyes and quickly pulled CoCo down towards me so that I could kiss her. Her pussy felt so warm and gushy, and it took everything in me not to come already. This was exactly why her ass ended up pregnant whenever we fucked around. Wasn't no way I was ever pulling out as long as the pussy was always this fire. CoCo's box had my toes curling up and my knees shaking and going weak.

"Fuck, baby," I grunted.

"This is not supposed to feel this good," CoCo said, a moan escaping right after.

"It is baby. We can do this all day every day. You know me. Just know you gon' stay with a gut full of Goat."

"You wish," CoCo chuckled as she slowly slid up and down on me.

"Fuck, I'm about to nut already." I shook my head and buried my face into CoCo's titties.

"Me too," she said and before I knew it, we were coming together.

. . .

Shit like this I could get used to. Hawaii was a beautiful ass place with good vibes and a dope ass scene. A nigga was thinking about taking all my kids and moving to an island. They done fucked around and showed a trapper the good life.

21

AHMEEN

The following Morning...

"Look, baby, they're getting married," Poe said as she stood out on the balcony of our hotel.

I got up from the bed and walked over to where she was. We had a big ass suite that was overlooking the ocean and from where we were standing, we could see down onto the beach. The sun had just come up not even an hour ago, and already someone was getting married.

"We need to get married wherever Wakanda took place," I told Poe before I smacked her on the ass.

"Boy shut up. I heard it took place in Atlanta, like everything else." She laughed and looked back at me.

"Shit, let me find out. That's what I want. All my niggas to be standing up on them rocks, and when you walk out, we all gonna say, Wakanda Forever!" I yelled all loud and shit causing everyone that was outside to look up at me. Poe smacked me, and I grabbed her and pulled her inside. "Come here."

"Noooooo, we are not about to have sex again," Poe protested and jerked her arm away from me.

"I ain't trying to have sex, big headed ass girl, and if I was, you was gon' give me some," I told her and she shook her head.

I sat down on the bed and pulled her between my legs. Looking up at her, I ran my hand down the side of her face and then placed kisses on her little pudge. She was almost three months along, and just like I had promised, I got her ass pregnant again.

"Just know that when these babies come, I'm getting my tubes tied," Poe said and I shook my head.

"Nahhh, you gotta give me one more and then we can be done."

"No, Ahmeen, I'm exhausted. I feel like I didn't even have a chance to breathe before I was pregnant again."

"I'mma let you breathe after the twins, I promise," I lied and kissed her stomach again. "But stop tripping man. I told you I'mma give you your dream wedding soon. Just been busy as fuck trying to get shit in order."

"Right..." Poe said and rolled her eyes.

"For real, if your ass knew you was gon' throw that shit in my fuckin' face every day then you should've never did that shit. I ain't put a gun to your head."

"I didn't say that you did, but I told you that I wanted to have a wedding, and every time I try to make a date, you tell me no. I'm starting to feel like you don't even care."

"To be honest with you, no I don't care. That wedding shit is for show. For muh'fuckas to spend money to impress other muh'fuckas. Only thing that I care about is you and making you happy. If you wanna have a big ass, over the top wedding then cool, whatever. Just give me time."

Poe pushed away from me and walked back towards the balcony. I shook my head before I grabbed my phone up from the nightstand and went inside of the bathroom. Two months ago, when we went to Vegas, I convinced Poe to go to the wedding chapel with me. She told me only if I gave her, her dream wedding and I promised that I would.

Only thing was, every month she chose, I had some major shit going on and felt like it wasn't the best time. She was all in her feelings about it saying that she wanted to do it as soon as possible before she got big with the twins. I really wasn't sweating that shit. Weddings were for females. I got what I wanted and that was for Poe to be my wife, but I wasn't going to be selfish. I was gon find the best time to clear my schedule, so she could have what she wanted and stop being so petty every time she saw somebody getting married.

"Sup..." I said into the receiver.

"You have been avoiding me," Javier said, and I sucked my teeth.

"Nah...just been busy, but I told you I got you. Soon as I get home, shit should be handled. I'll let you know when it's done," I told him and sucked in a deep breath.

"You told me the same thing months ago. How do I know that I can trust your word?"

"You and I both know that Maino is very smart. Finding him out in the open and not ready ain't gon' happen, but like I said, it's gon be handled. The nigga will be dead before the end of next week, I promise you that. You just be ready to do what you supposed to do."

I pulled the phone away from my ear and noticed that he had hung up on me. I had been doing my best to leave that nigga Maino be hoping that Javier or either Mario would catch up to him, and I didn't have to get my hands dirty at all. It was obvious they wanted me to do their dirty work. I knew I had to do something though and soon.

Poe didn't know, but the only reason I had up and took this sudden trip to Hawaii was because Latrel told me he'd spotted Mario following her in the grocery store one day. I didn't want to spook her, and Latrel had it handled, but I knew it was best for me to move around until Maino was gone. My connect to him had hit me this morning and let me know that everything was a go and they was ready to set things in motion. So this was what it was gon' be. Either Maino or Poe.

22

MAINO

Moving Day...

Ding Dong! Ding Dong!

"Who the hell is that?" I said before dropping a few items into a box.

Finally, after a few months of looking, we had finally gotten a spot where I was comfortable with moving. It wasn't where Toya had originally wanted, but it was right in between Memphis and Gatlinburg. I was trying real hard, but wasn't quite ready to let the streets go all together. Sam and I did good business and ran up big bags. With her product, and my hustle, I was ready to go down to the hoods of Memphis and flood that thang with all white.

Chuck and Tyree were moving with me, and I was even trying to convince my pops to pack up and leave, too, but he was stuck. He was too worried about leaving Poe behind, but like me, he was gonna have to come to the realization that baby girl was gon' live her life.

Shawty's nigga had ran up in my spot, fought me, and had his men even put a gun to my head and she had gone back to him that same night. I wasn't mad at her but had to see that she was gon' always love the nigga she was fucking above all else no matter what he put her through. It took me realizing that it was the same way with Toya for me to see it for myself. Toya loved me down to my dirty drawers and always forgave me no matter how many times I fucked up. For that reason, I was leaving Poe to do what she was gon' do. Long as she knew that I was always here for her whenever she needed me.

"Who is it?" I yelled out before I looked through the peephole. "Speak of the devil."

Pulling the door open, I smiled when I saw Poe standing on the other side with her fat ass baby on her hip. I reached out and took him from her before turning around to walk inside to finish packing. We had a couple of hours before the movers showed up and I wanted to be ready to go and get on the road when they arrived.

"Damn, you can't speak to me," Poe commented, and I looked back at her.

"Sup...what you doing here?" I asked her before going to where I was.

"You don't want me over here now?"

"I never know when I see you if I'mma be ducking and dodging bullets or not. Don't be knowing how to take your presence no more. I'm happy to see you, though," I told her and she pursed her lips together. "You pregnant again?"

"...yea, I am."

I shook my head but didn't say anything. Sitting on the arm of the couch, I kissed Little Man before holding him up in the air. He giggled while slob dripped from his mouth onto my face. I chuckled before wiping it away and kissing him on the cheeks.

"Why does it look like you're leaving?" Poe asked while looking around.

"Maino, you didn't tell Poe we were moving," Toya said as she wobbled into the living room carrying a few pillows.

"Thought your ass was working and you come down here carrying pillows," I cracked and she chuckled.

"I was working. I packed up all my makeup and hair supplies. The movers can do the rest. I'm tired," Toya said before sitting in the recliner.

"Moving where?" Poe asked, and I looked at her.

"To Tennessee."

"Huh? Why?"

"Because it's time for me to go. Gotta find a place for the kids, somewhere I ain't gotta worry about a lot of bullshit," I told Poe and she nodded before looking around.

"Well...I need to tell you something. Can we go somewhere and talk in private?"

I looked at Poe and could tell that something was bothering her. Nodding my head, I waved for her to follow me to the kitchen while wondering what was going on with her ass now. It wasn't until we had gotten inside of the kitchen and under better lighting that I noticed that she had been crying about something.

"What that nigga do to you now?" I asked and she shook her head while fidgeting with her hands.

"We just got back into town this morning, and I have been dying to get over here hoping that it wasn't too late," Poe said and I eyed her before placing Little Man over my shoulder and patting him on the back.

"I overheard Ahmeen talking to the Mexican Cartel. I don't know what they were saying to him, but I know he was telling them that he was going to handle you when he got back. He doesn't know that I overheard him, but I think it's supposed to happen tonight," Poe said and I sighed.

"Happen by who? Your nigga?"

"I don't know," Poe said, tears falling from her eyes. "He just told them that you wasn't an easy person to catch and that you was always already. I don't know if he's supposed to be doing something or somebody else, Maino. I don't want you to leave, but it's probably the best thing."

I chuckled. "Right, while you stay with the nigga that's supposed to kill me. You funny as fuck man. Thank you for the info baby sis, but I'm good."

Knock Knock Knock! Ding Dong! Ding Dong!

"Emmanuel, don't do that. Don't act like I don't care. That's why I came over here...I promise you, if I didn't care, I wouldn't have come here and told you this. I just want all this stop."

"Yea, what the fuck ever. Preciate it, but I'm good," I waved her off and started to walk away, when Toya started yelling.

"Mainoooooo!"

I quickly handed Poe's baby to her and took off running towards the front of the house. When I looked in the living room, she was no longer sitting in the recliner like she had been before I walked out. I then walked into the dining area before I heard yelling again.

"Bitch you better be glad that I'm pregnant hoe! You bitches is really bold," Toya yelled and I rushed up behind her as she stood in the doorway.

"What the fuck going on?" I asked her before I pulled the door open and saw Sam standing there.

"Sorry, I tried calling, texting you and all that letting you know that I needed to talk to you, but like you said, don't bother you if wasn't concerning business," Sam said before she held out a pregnancy test and tried to hand it to me.

I jumped back like the bitch had a handful of fire while mugging her. I knew this hoe was playing games because I hadn't touched her in months and I always strapped up every time we fucked.

"Really, Maino. Again?" Toya said and I looked at her and frowned.

"Mannnnn," I drawled and then sighed. "Sam, why the fuck you lying yo. You know damn well you ain't pregnant by me. Hoe I ain't touched you in months!"

"And nigga I'm almost four months along. Like I told you, I been trying to tell you, but you wanted to be difficult so it what it is. I just figured you would like to know that you're about to be a daddy...

again," Samantha commented, before she tossed the pregnancy test to her feet and walked away.

"I'm done. Swear to God, I'm done," Toya said before she pushed past me and walked away.

"Toya, chill. I swear on everything that hoe ain't pregnant by me." I slammed the door shut and followed behind her.

"Maino, how the fuck you know? It's the fact that not even a whole year later, here we go again. You gon' kill her too. Leave her body behind and have us running from whoever care about her too," Toya said, causing me to look at her oddly as I wondered how she knew all that. "Yea nigga, I'm not as dumb as I pretend to be. I know about Eve. I know she was pregnant. Dumb ass nigga when she was playing on my phone, she told me that she was pregnant and that she was keeping it. Then all of a sudden things go quiet, I don't hear from her ass anymore, and I look up and see someone posted a RIP message to her on Facebook and not long after that you're telling me we gotta go and leave everything behind! It don't take a rocket scientist to put two and two together. I'm tired Maino. I can't take this shit anymore. We have two fucking daughters who can't even have a stable home because of your shit and then we about to bring two more into the same shit. I can't do it anymore."

"I know, Toya, I'm sorry. I fucked up, but I promise you all that shit is over. That's why I wanna move, so we can start over. I'm done fucking up. I put that on my kids I am," I pleaded with her as tears ran down her eyes.

"Why you couldn't be done the last time huh? You really got me up in here about to lose our kids behind your bullshit and you're still out there fooling around. It's cool, Maino. You can have this life and the hoes that come with it since that's all you seem to care about. I'm done. I'm done. I'm done," Toya cried, before she shoved me in the chest and turned around to walk away.

Poe glared at me before she went after Toya. I ran my hand down my face and took in deep breaths trying to get myself to calm down, but I couldn't. I knew this hoe Sam was lying. I sucked my teeth, before I blacked out and ran out of the house and headed towards this bitch's condo.

I wasn't gon' kill this bitch because I truly did learn from the last time, but I was gon' beat her to the point that she wished that she was dead. Yea, I knew that I shouldn't have played with her feelings, but this was taking it too far. If it had been true that was one thing but making up a lie and bringing the shit to my doorstep was real fucked up.

I probably had made it to Sam's crib in less than twenty minutes with the way I was flying down the highway. I got out and went through the lobby and bypassed the elevator so that I could quickly take the stairs. Once I made it up to the floor she lived on, I pushed through the door and went to her apartment.

BAM! BAM! BAM!

"Open up this muh'fuckin' door!" I yelled and stepped back.

BAM! BAM! BAM!

I drew my foot back and kicked the door open, not giving a fuck who around this bitch heard me. Going inside, I went room for room looking for her, but didn't see her anywhere. I should've known her bird ass wasn't going to be here though after pulling that shit.

Sucking my teeth, I left out of the apartment and went back down to my car. I was gonna wait the bitch out for however long it took. She had to come home at some point, and I had time today.

I opened the door to my car and fell inside of the driver's seat. Pulling the middle console open, I grabbed a cigar and then opened the glove department to grab my sack of weed. I gutted the cigar and licked the insides before breaking the weed down and filling it up.

"Gon' head and get your last high in, my dude," I heard from behind me and my heart dropped.

I froze as I veered through the rearview mirror only to see a set of eyes staring back at me. I couldn't tell who it was because of the hoodie they were wearing, and it was dark as fuck in the parking garage. But from the sound of his voice, it sounded like Ahmeen.

"Shit...nigga got caught slipping," I said, and finished rolling my blunt.

"It happens to the best of us. I really was trying to let your ass make it cause I swear your sister will never forgive me for this shit," the nigga said, confirming his identity. "But that nigga Mario on her head for some shit you caused. So, they told me it's either her or you, so what the fuck am I supposed to do? Not like I was gonna choose you, especially since not long ago, they had you coming for me. Sounds like it was a lose, lose situation regardless and she gotta be there for our kids, so I'm sure you understand."

"Definitely," I told him and lit the blunt. "I would've done the same thing. So that was you dropping them notes and shit?"

"Nah...wrong enemy nigga."

I ran my hand down my face and when I looked through my front window, I spotted Sam's car pulling into a parking spot. She hopped out and looked back at me. Our eyes met, and she smirked before waving her hand at me and then turning to walk way. At that point, I realized that she had set me up.

"Aye, take care of my sister. For whatever reason, she love your ass, but just look out for her. She a good girl," I told Ahmeen while I put the blunt out.

"I know, and I love her too, but trust I got you," he replied and I nodded.

"Do me a solid and let me call my girl if you don't mind," I asked and veered at him through the rearview mirror.

He nodded his head and I slowly went into my pocket and pulled out my phone. A nigga really wanted to reach for the burner that I had on the side of my seat but knew I wouldn't be quick enough. Ahmeen was ready with his finger on the trigger and would have a bullet in me before I could even get my hands on it good enough. Something told me when I had pulled up to grab it, but I didn't wanna be tempted to murk Sam's ass. Grimy bitch.

"Bae, I know you mad at a nigga, but just know that I love you with everything in me. I might not have been the perfect nigga, but you was always the perfect woman for me. Sometimes it takes men to damn near lose it all before they finally get it together. I swear the day we went to the movies was the best day of my life. I ain't even wanna see that shit, but you pressed and pressed and I was glad I did. That movie did something to a nigga and it made me think about everything that I had been tripping on. Anyway, later on, you'll see that hoe Sam was lying and did all that shit for a reason. I always knew that my ways was gon' catch back up to me. I'm just mad that we wasn't on good terms when it did. But always and forever you and my kids will be good. I didn't get to meet my boys, but please tell them daddy loves them and did everything he did for a reason," I said into Toya's voicemail.

Soon as I ended the call and laid the phone down on the middle console, the shot went off. I was so cool and calm about it all that I didn't even feel anything when the bullet left the chamber. I had long ago accepted that the streets was always gon' come back to haunt you. Them tables was always turning.

23

POETIC

1 week later...

"Aghh...agghhhhh!" I screamed, while burying my head into the side of the pillow as tears raced down my face.

"Damn, can y'all give her something else for the pain? Damn this shit already hard enough," Ahmeen yelled out and tried to grab my hand, but I snatched it away from him.

"Don't touch me! Don't ever fuckin' put your hands on me again!" I told him, wishing he would just leave me alone.

Everything from the middle of my back down to my pussy was hurting. I didn't even remember being in this much pain when I had gone into labor with Jr, but this here was far worse. Last night, I had come home late after spending the entire day with my mom, daddy, Tyree, Chuck, Herbo, and Toya and the kids at the funeral and then repass for Maino. I thought that burying Melody was the hardest day of my life, but I had to admit that this had been worse than anything I had felt.

Probably because I knew that the man that I had chosen to love, marry, and have a child with was the person responsible. Whether he had done it himself or had someone else to do it, I knew that he was behind it. I heard him while he was in Hawaii telling that guy that he was going to handle it and he fucking did.

I tried to be calm. I tried to let it go. I tried to tell myself that maybe Maino was finally getting payback for killing Ahmeen's mother, but he didn't know that. Ahmeen still thought that Quavo killed Mrs. Shakur. Him killing Maino was something that he had going on with the fucking Cartel and something he had been wanting to do.

Knowing that made me angry, and I started fighting Ahmeen. I threw shit at him, and hit him with whatever I could get my hands on. Not one time did he hit me back or even try to stop me from hurting him. He knew he was guilty, and he knew that what he did would hurt me, but he had done it anyway. Ahmeen just didn't give a fuck about nobody but himself and that was obvious to me.

Just like last time, I made him think things were calm with us, but this time when I tried to sneak away it was the worst mistake that I had ever made. I ended up tripping over my own feet and fell down the entire flight of stairs in our home one by one.

Now here I was at the hospital with a broken arm and forced to deliver two dead babies. I had killed my own kids and it was something that I was going to have to live with for the rest of my life. I blamed Ahmeen, too, but I knew that had I moved differently, I wouldn't be here today.

"I guess you blaming me for this too, right?" Ahmeen had the nerve to ask and I reached over and grabbed a glass and chunked it at him.

He ducked down just in time causing it to hit my room door and shatter into pieces. I looked at him, my chest heaving up and down from all the anger and pain that I had inside of me. I should've known better. I should've known that me and him could never work.

"When this is over, I want you to take me to my parents' house and to never speak to me again. I want a divorce. I don't want to ever even see you again," I told him.

"Here you go with that bullshit again, but you got it, Poe. It's always whatever you want," Ahmeen said and I winced when another contraction hit.

"How is it whatever I want? Huh?" I said and suddenly screamed out again. I gripped my stomach and waited and waited for the pain to surpass. "You killed my brother, Ahmeen. You knew that it would hurt me, and you did it anyway. You told me that you would never do anything to hurt me again. And don't lie because I heard you in Hawaii. You told them that soon as we got back you was going to handle him."

"Yea, but you know so much right? Shut the fuck up talking to me. I ain't gotta explain myself to you. You want a divorce, I'll give you one. Not tryna wife a chick that wanna run off every time shit get tough any fucking way. Take your ass back to your people and see if I give a fuck!" Ahmeen spat, and I stared at him in disgust.

"Of course, you don't care. Only person you care about is you. Selfish ass. Wish they would've locked your ass up. Wish they would've convicted you and we wouldn't even be here today," I told him, and he shook his head and came towards me.

"Yea, maybe if they had locked me up, your muh'fuckin' ass will be dead right now since they was coming at your ass for some shit your brother did. Dumb ass girl. Fuck you think I keep your stupid ass in the house or always got somebody on you when you leave. Protecting your retarded ass for some shit that ain't even have nothing to do with me, but you got it man for real. Talk your shit. Soon as this shit over with, you ain't gotta worry about me ever again unless it concerns my son."

I started to say something further but didn't. I thought about what he was saying and wondered if it had any truth to it. Ahmeen had never talked to me like this. Not even when I cussed him out, and talked to him sideways, he would never get this out of pocket with me. I looked him over and just settled into the hospital bed, doing my best to get through these contractions until it was time to deliver my babies.

Regardless of what happened, I know that this was just as hard on him as it was for me. He had been happier about me being pregnant than I had. For now, I was going to chill out and make it through this. After it was over, I would figure out what happened to my brother.

24

AHMEEN

Eight Months later…

"Da-Da-Da-Da," Jr. said as he held his arms out for me.

"Meen, are we there yet? I feel like I'm going to fall and break my damn neck," Poe whined, just as I scooped my little one up from the ground, and then placed my hand onto Poe's back.

She was wearing a blind fold and taking little baby steps at a time. Had her ass put on some tennis shoes and not the four-inch stilettos she was wearing, she probably could walk faster.

"Step up," I told her after I had unlocked the door and then pushed it open.

I helped her inside and then flicked the switch on that turned on all of the lights. Sitting Jr down on the floor, I stepped behind Poe and then pulled the blindfold off of her. She knew a nigga like me loved surprises. Regardless if we were together or not, I told her that I had something that was going to make up for all my bullshit and still had followed through on that. I had taken damn near a year to see it through, but now that it was done, I couldn't wait to present it to her. I knew none of it could ever bring her brother back or even fix the heartbreak that I had caused her, but hopefully she would see that no matter what I was a nigga that stood behind his word.

"Ahmeen...why do you always do this to me?" Poe said, her hands coming to her face as she looked around, her eyes froze on the logo that was sitting on top of a picture of her sister Melody. "The 3 B's."

"Bundles, Brows, and Boutique. That's all I used to hear you talk about. 'Woo, Meen, I want to go get my brows done. Aww baby, I just found me some good ass bundles. I think I wanna open up my own boutique'," I said mocking her voice and the shit she used to always talk about.

One thing I knew about Poe was that she was used to shit. She was used to somebody always giving her something, always putting money in her pocket, designer on her body, and a bunch of other shit. I was trying to give her something that she would have to make her own. I bought her the building, but it was up to her to make it excel and be successful. From there, she could expand and open up spots all over Atlanta and in different states.

"Why would you do this for me?"

"Shit, you the mother of my child...and hell, still my wife at the end of the day. Regardless of what we going through, I always want you and my little one to be good," I told her and she started to walk around.

"Wow...I don't even know what to say right now. Besides, thank you, Meen. This really means a lot to me. You of all people know how bad I been struggling and trying to find a way to stand on my own, and this just really did it for me," Poe said, her voice cracking as she spoke.

"Get on top of it then. Everything in your name. Got your keys right here, and even got you a marketing firm ready to get you started for the next few months. Ain't nothing you can't do baby, and you know that."

Poe rushed over to me and wrapped her arms around me. She held onto me for a long while before looking up at me and smiling. I leaned over and kissed her on the forehead before pushing her away. I ain't even like to do all that mushy shit with her no more, because at the end of the night, her and my son was going one place and I was going another.

After she had given birth to the twins, she claimed she had forgiven me for the Maino situation, but she really didn't. All we did was fight with her blaming me for every little thing. She kept putting her hands on me every time she got mad, and I was doing everything I could to keep my cool. Shit got so bad that I just stopped coming home. I found myself back in the streets with a new chick every night the same way I had been when I was with Kiani.

Eventually, I grew tired of it all and just ended it. I allowed Poe to keep the house and I moved back in with my pops until I figured out what I wanted to do. Whenever I went to spend time with my lil one, we always ended up fucking around and that shit only kept the both of us lingering behind. My feelings for her were still deep as fuck and I doubted anything would ever change that. Her fucking around with another nigga would kill me, but I knew at some point I was gonna have to let her go.

"You got my message I sent you this morning about tonight?" I asked Poe and she looked at me and rolled her eyes.

"Yea of course I'm going. I just gotta see if your daddy or my mom can watch Jr for us, but yes I'm going to be there," she said, and I nodded.

"Cool, yea see if your people can get him because my pops gon' be there, too. You want me to pick you up or you gon' drive?"

"I prefer for you to pick me up, but I know you said that you wasn't trying to come to the house like that no more," Poe said and I nodded.

"It's cool, I'll come. Well, shit, here go your keys. Let me know if you need me for anything and I got you," I told her and handed over the keys to the building.

"Thank you again, Meen. It really means a lot to me."

"Say less," I told her, before kissing her forehead. "Come here give daddy a hug."

I held my hands out for Jr and he came running to me. Leaning down to pick him up, I tossed him in the air a few times before planting kisses all over his face. He giggled and threw his head back, and I started tickling him and blowing bubbles on his little stomach.

"Love you. I love you fat man. Give daddy kiss," I told him, and he pecked my jaw leaving all his slob behind. "See you tonight."

I sat him on the ground before leaving the two of them behind. I had to get ready for my boy's little dinner party tonight. Goat and CoCo had gotten engaged and were planning to get married in a few weeks. I was the best man and CoCo had asked for Poe to be one of her bridesmaids. The two of them had gotten real close and did just about everything together. That was one of the other things that made it hard for the both of us to even move on. If Poe's ass wasn't always at the house with my pops and his girl, she was at Goat's chilling with CoCo. We were always running into other. Out of respect, I never brought another female around, and of course she wasn't bringing no dude 'round my people. Both of their ass would be just as good as dead.

I climbed the stairs and didn't even knock before I pushed open the bedroom door and went inside. Poe stood in front of the full-length mirror with nothing on but her bra and panties and I shook my head knowing that her ass wasn't going to be ready. It always took her hours to do her hair, makeup and to find something to wear. She was never on time for shit, which was why I was glad that Goat and CoCo told me that they were running behind and had to push the dinner back and hour. I didn't tell Poe that though cause she wouldn't do shit but use that hour to take even more time and still end up late.

"Your ass ain't never ready," I told her before walking over to the bed and crashing on it.

"I'm almost ready. Haven't been feeling good, so I just got out of bed an hour ago. I'm not even going to do my hair or make-up. I feel horrible," Poe said and I peeked at her from behind.

"What's wrong with you? You seemed fine earlier."

"Nothing. A cold I guess," she said, and I nodded.

"Stay home. I'll go get Jr when I leave."

"No, CoCo will kill me if I don't come."

I got up and went into the bathroom so that I could take a piss. I had drunk a couple of beers with pops earlier and that shit had been running through me ever since. I raised the seat to the toilet up, and then whipped my dick out. Soon as I was done peeing, I went to wash my hands and noticed an empty pregnancy test box sitting next to the sink.

"Ughhhh," Poe commented as she stood in the doorway.

I glared at her before I dried my hands off and then walked over to the small wastebasket that sat near the toilet. Inside of it was a pregnancy test. The two lines on it confirmed that the test had been positive. I shook my head and sighed before I brushed past her and walked out of the bathroom.

"I'll be outside in the car," I told her.

"So, you're not going to say anything?"

"Fuck you want me to say?" I stopped and turned to face her.

"Something. Do you want me to keep it, get an abortion? What?"

"Shit is it mine?" I asked, and she cocked her head to the side and stared at me like I was crazy.

"Don't fuckin' insult me. Unlike you, I ain't been with nobody else."

"Well nah, I don't want you to keep it. I asked your ass was you on birth control and you told me yes, so how this happen?"

"You want me to get an abortion," Poe said on the verge of tears.

I sighed and ran my hand down my face. Had me and Poe been together, I wouldn't have given a damn how many times she had gotten pregnant. I always had wanted a big, close family, but not like this. All this back and forth shit with me seeing my kid when I had time was for the fuckin' birds. Wasn't no way I was trying to bring another kid into a fucked up situation. I wasn't one for abortion, but it was better than this shit.

"After the babies we lost, you really want me to get a fuckin' abortion?"

"I ain't trying to raise no kids in a broken fuckin home! My son barely fuckin' know me because I can't see him like I want to."

"I never stopped you from seeing him, Meen."

I shook my head and turned around to leave. Poe rushed to stop me. She stepped in front of me and pushed me back. Her eyes held a desperate look, and I took in a deep breath before letting it all out again. I knew her ass was about to try to fight me. Seemed like, now that was all she knew how to do to express herself was get physical.

"Don't put your hands on me, Poe."

"I'm not, Ahmeen. Just wait a minute, please," Poe pleaded. "I miss you soooo much. I understand everything. I know that you did what you did to protect me, but I was so hurt back then, and I know that I pushed you away. So much has happened to me over the past few years that I didn't even know who I was anymore. I took a lot of shit out on you and you was so patient with me and I thank you for that. You see that I never pushed for the divorce or any of that. I never wanted us to be apart and earlier when I found out that I was pregnant, I was thinking that maybe this was our angel baby. The baby that would bring us back together."

"Took you all this time and a pregnancy to realize that?"

"You know that I can be stubborn sometimes, but truthfully, I wanted to get myself together. I been so messed up, but nobody could fix me but me. I had to get my mind right so that I can be a better mother and a better wife. I know you've noticed I've been calling you over here for Jr a lot lately. Been wanting to see you and spend time with you, but just didn't know how to tell you."

Poe came closer to me and wrapped her arms around me. She buried her head against my stomach and just held onto me but didn't say anything. I ain't even know if this was good or bad. More than anything, I wanted my family. I never not wanted to be with Poe, but it was the bullshit and all the drama that came with her that I couldn't deal with. If she was ready though, then I was more than ready to fix everything.

25

GOAT

"Oh, my God, I can't believe that we have a week and a half left before we are getting married," CoCo beamed, and I looked over at her and chuckled.

"I can't believe it either. I'm ready though. I feel like we should've moved first. That damn house seems like it's getting smaller and smaller by the day," I told her before I pulled up to the house I used to share with Jyelle.

We had just come back from the dinner party we threw for all of our family to celebrate our engagement and upcoming wedding. Everything had gone by so fast considering I didn't propose to CoCo until the day she had given birth to our daughter GiGi a little over a month ago. I was ready to go to the courthouse the next day and be done with it, but CoCo had wanted a wedding. I told her she had two months and she got with Poe and made shit happen. Here we were ready to walk down the aisle together in less than two weeks, and I was ready to get it over with.

Nobody could've ever told me I would be here, getting ready to marry my first baby mama. The chick I had dogged out so many times that it was a wonder she had any love for me left. I had done some of the most unthinkable things to her, but she had never folded on me. Sometimes it really took a muthafucka to experience all the fake and the bullshit before they realized that what they had all along was real.

"Give me a kiss," I told my daughter Jy'Asia soon as she undid her seatbelt.

She kissed me on the cheek and hurried up and climbed out of the car. I hopped out before she could get away and grabbed her arm to stop her. She looked back at me and rolled her eyes. Jy'Asia was my second oldest child that I had with Jyelle. I was only sixteen when she had been born and her ass was already about to be nine years old. I felt like if I closed my eyes too long, she was going to be a teenager with little boys running around behind her. She had her mama's attitude and the shit drove me crazy cause more than any of my kids, I had to stay on her the most.

"What the hell is going on with you? You ain't gonna tell Ms. CoCo bye or your brother and sister?" I asked her just as Germaine and Jr got out of the car.

"Bye," Jy'Asia waved, her attitude on real thick and strong. She jerked away from me before running in the house. "Come on Germaine and Jr.!"

"Bye daddy, she always acts like that now," Jr told me before he gave me a hug.

"Oh yea, why is that? Did I do something to her?"

"She's mad that we can't come and stay with you like Gem and Giaria. She said that mama boyfriend came in her room and now she's all scared of him," Germaine said and my heart dropped.

"Mama boyfriend? Came in her room and did what?" I asked, and both of the boys shrugged.

"Go get back in the car," I told them, before I sucked my teeth.

"Why? I thought..."

"I said get in the fuckin' car!"

"Babe, what's wrong?" CoCo asked getting out of the car.

"Talking about something about Jy boyfriend going in Asia room. I'mma be right back," I told her and stormed towards the house.

Before I could even go inside, Jyelle was stepping outside pulling

Jy'Asia along with her. I glared down at the front of her clothes and saw that she had blood everywhere. Her eyes were spaced out and she didn't even look like herself.

"I need...I need for you to take them. You know take care of them now. I'm probably going to go to jail now," Jyelle told me, tears running down her face.

"Huh...what the fuck?" I asked her, before I brushed past her and went inside of the house.

I looked around until I hit the hallway and spotted some big nigga with a bullet in the center of his forehead. My eyes bucked and I quickly backed away before running outside to where CoCo was trying to comfort Jyelle. I was confused as fuck right now.

"What the fuck happened? You shot that nigga? Who the fuck is that?"

"He touched my baby! He touched her! I saw him in there last night and this morning I saw her panties on the floor with blood in them! I asked him about it today and he told me that she wanted it. You gotta take them for me, Goat. CoCo, please?" Jyelle begged before more tears ran down her face. "I'm not well anyway. You know, it's my fault. I should've never brought him around her, but I been sick you know?"

"I got them..." I told her, knowing exactly what she meant by sick. "CoCo get them to the house and I'll be there later."

"Goat?" CoCo questioned before she stood up from where Jyelle was and rushed over to me. "What are you about to do?"

"I'm not about to let my baby mama go down for murdering no pussy ass pedophile. Better be glad she got to his ass first, fuck that. Take them home and I'll be there later," I urged, and she grimaced before she turned around and went to the car.

I helped Jyelle up from the ground and we both went inside. One thing I didn't do was play about my family, especially not my mutha-fucking kids. Me and Jyelle didn't have the best relationship, but one thing was for certain that she was the mother of my kids. She stepped up and did what she had to do to protect our daughter, so I was gonna step in and protect her. Wasn't no way I would let her go down for no shit like this.

26

POETIC

D ays later...

Soon as I left CoCo's dinner the other night, I immediately started doing my research to find all the vendors that I needed to get things up and popping. I had to find the perfect hair vendor, a vendor for the clothing, and then take the classes that I needed so that I could get my license together to do brows.

For now, though, I had already listed the building as a place that had space available for rent. I had a total of fifteen open rooms that me and CoCo had been here all day decorating them so that they would be presentable when people came to view the spaces. I knew it was going to take time, but I could already see how dope it was going to be.

Meen just didn't know what he had done for me. I had always wanted to stand on my own and set myself apart from being the daughter of the infamous Noie King or now the wife of the great Ahmeen Shakur. I wanted people to know me as me, and that was as Poetic King-Shakur. I was a smart girl with a good head on her shoulders that was now a fucking business owner.

Pretty soon, I would be having beauticians, lash techs, brow techs, estheticians and more, renting a space in my building while I was selling bundles, clothes and doing brows myself. It wouldn't be long before I expanded and made the The 3B's known as a worldwide entity.

"Sooo what did Ahmeen say? You've been hella quiet over there. It don't take that much concentration to paint a wall," CoCo said, and I glared at her.

"He told me that he wanted me to start counseling and that eventually he wanted us to go as a family. He's like he's tired of every time I get mad or throw a fit that I either want to break up or I try running away from him. He said that all the fighting we had done for those months had really fucked him up. I said and did a lot of messed up stuff and I really hurt him. He just doesn't feel like I'm ready and don't want to mess up what we have left of us by rushing into it," I told her, and she walked over to where I was standing on the ladder.

"And how did that make you feel? Do you agree?" she asked, and I wished that I could speak on Maino so that she could know everything.

"I am hurt...but I do understand where he is coming from. I belittled him. I called him all kinds of names. I talked down on him every chance I could and even too many times told him I wish he was either dead or in jail. Not even just that, I put my hands on him so much that I'm surprised that I'm not somewhere dead. I did so much until he just couldn't take it anymore and I don't blame him. I know I can't expect that now that I am ready and feel better that he's just going to take me back and things will be back to normal," I said a tear sliding down my face.

"Awwww, don't cry Pooh," CoCo said and reached up to rub my back.

I swear I loved CoCo. She was eight years older than me, and we had become friends by default. Now we were almost inseparable, with her being like the big sister I never had. Without her, I didn't know how I would make it through Maino's death. She would come and see me just about every other day when I was going through. She would cook, clean up my house, and just keep me company all while she was pregnant and taking care of her own kids. I loved her so much and I could tell that she loved me too.

"One thing I know is that Ahmeen hasn't been the same since you two split. He used to talk about you all the time and now it's like he's lost without you. Knowing that, I know that things will come full circle and that y'all will work it out. It's going to take time, but girl when it's meant to be then it will be. Shit, look at me and Goat."

I chuckled and shook my head.

"Yea, I know you're right. It just scares me to think that he's going to one day tell me that he's not interested in fixing it and that he found someone better. I know he's out here dealing with chicks and I just gotta deal with it."

"Helllooooo!"

CoCo and I both looked around after hearing a voice that was coming from the front of the building. I carefully climbed down off the ladder and then placed the paintbrush I had been holding into the bucket. We walked out of the suite we had been directing and made our way to the front. Seeing my old best friend Tyese standing there with some flowers in her hand had taken me by surprise. I smiled slightly wondering what she was doing there. I hadn't seen her in almost two years and the last time I had, she was coming at me on some jealousy shit that made me feel like I couldn't trust her.

"Ummm... dang girl. Surprised to see you. Then you bring flowers," I told her, as she handed me a vase with a huge smile on her face.

"Girl, I wish I had been that thoughtful, but they're not for me. A guy handed them to me when I was walking in," Tyese said.

"Oh..." I took the vase and sat them down in the area where I was trying to decide if I was going to make it a reception desk or a cash register. I noticed that there was a card attached to the arraignment, so I pulled it off and read the note.

Baby Girl,
    Since I couldn't come and tell you in person, just thought I'd send you

my love to let you know I was thinking of you. I'm proud of you and how far you've come. Keep it up and see you soon. Love You.

The note didn't say who it was from, but I assumed that it was from Ahmeen. He was the only person besides CoCo that had been telling me how proud they were of me. I pulled my cell phone out and went to text Meen to let him know I received them and a thank you. He was always doing something special for me and that was something that I would truly miss if we didn't get this shit together.

Me: *Thank you for the roses. I appreciate them. Love you.*

Hubby: *I ain't sent you no damn flowers. Don't make me come fuck you up. You got some nigga sending you roses????*

Me: *Lol stop playing. Tyese brought them in. Nigga I just read the note and no I don't talk to no one but you.*

Hubby: *Yea, I'm on my way. Got me fucked up.*

Me: *Seriously? You didn't send me no flowers?*

Hubby: *I just said I didn't. Let me find out you fucking around.*

Me: *We would have to be in a relationship for me to be fucking around. Last time I checked you told me I wasn't ready.*

Hubby: *Still my wife. But say less.*

Hubby: *Who the hell is Tyese?*

Me: *That girl I used to be cool with back when you and I first met.*

Hubby: *Ohhh the girl that used to clown you with your sister. Get that bitch gone. Latrel still outside?*

I looked up to see if Latrel was still outside and his truck was indeed parked out front of the building. He had been sitting there all damn day too. Of all the men that worked for Ahmeen, he had become my favorite and the only person that was trusted to watch over me and Jr.

Me: *Yea he still here. You know Latrel ain't going nowhere.*

Hubby: *Bet not. I'm on my way though for real. I got tickets to go to Wild N Out. Be there in like 10 minutes.*

Me: *K.*

Hubby: *Oh, I love you too fat face. Better throw them flowers in the fuckin' trash can too.*

I laughed before I slid my phone into my pocket and then took the flowers and placed them behind the counter where they couldn't be seen. I wasn't going to throw them away because I didn't know who they were from. It could've been from my daddy or either Chuck or Tyree so I would just check with them later.

"So what brings you by?" I asked Tyese, remembering that she was still standing there.

"I saw that you was advertising space on your IG and wanted to come by and check it out. You know I braid hair, and a having my own lil set up would be so bomb," Tyese said and I eyed her.

"Would you like me to show her the spaces?" CoCo asked and I bit down on the inside of my cheeks.

"They're not ready yet. That's why I said Monday that they would be available for viewing. I didn't want nobody coming when the shit was half done," I lied, knowing that me and CoCo only had two rooms left before we were done.

"Right..." CoCo caught on quick.

"And not only that, Meen is on his way to get me so I gotta lock up."

"Okay...well it's cool. I can just come back Monday. It was nice seeing you," Tyese told me and out of nowhere hugged me.

I gave her a quick hug back before I quickly pulled away from her. She walked out first and me and CoCo stayed back to tidy up the mess we had made before turning all the lights out and locking up to leave. It had been over ten minutes so I knew that Ahmeen should've been pulling up at any moment.

"Girl, I think you did right by listening to your gut and Ahmeen on that one? How she come down here talking about letting her see a space when the shit obviously said Monday," CoCo said, and I shook my head before laughing.

"Yea...I'mma listen on that one. She don't want shit but to be nosey any damn way. I guess she thought since she was cool before that she was gon get some kind of special treatment. Either way girl, it looks like that's Ahmeen, so I'mma call you later," I told CoCo and gave her a hug.

"Alright girl. And don't be getting all in your feelings. Give it time and everything gon' work out. I love you," she said before blowing me a kiss and walking away.

"I love you too! And thank you!"

CoCo waved me off and I turned around ready to walk to Ahmeen's car when a set of lights suddenly blinded me. I brought my hand up to shield my eyes to see what looked like my sister Lyric sitting in the driver's seat of a tan Ford Fusion. I furrowed my brows and when I noticed that it actually was her with Tyese sitting right beside her, I shook my head and started to walk off towards Ahmeen.

"Who the fuck is that?" he asked as I got ready to cross the street that led to the parking lot.

"It's Lyric and Tyese..." I told him just as the Ford Fusion sped up and came straight at me.

ERCHHHHHHHH!

EPILOGUE

Poe

Three months later...

I swear it seemed like nothing was going right today. Things were supposed to have started over an hour ago, but we had to get a damn seamstress here since my stomach seemed to want to grow overnight. Because I was frustrated, I had been crying, which forced my makeup artist to have to fix my face every few minutes. My hair kept falling, and at this point, I just wanted to say fuck it and not even do this anymore.

"Girl, look at me. Look at me," CoCo came over to me and placed both hands on the side of my face. "If you don't calm your little behind down you gonna stress everyone out. You got Ahmeen out there thinking that something is wrong. Stop worrying. You look beautiful, but the more you pick at shit, the more you gonna think something is wrong."

"Okay...okay," I said and took in a deep breath.

"Now when they cue this damn music, you better be walking your ass out this damn room. Your ass wanted to have a big wedding, so come on, Bridezilla," CoCo fussed, and I couldn't help but laugh.

"Ok, I'm coming," I sighed.

Yes! After all the bullshit. The deaths, the fussing, the back and forth, the running and everything else, me and Ahmeen were finally here having the dream wedding I had been wanting. The day that I left the shop and Lyric's dumb ass tried to kill me yet again was another fail. Unfortunately though, Latrel had jumped in front of me and took the impact of the car away. Ahmeen couldn't get to me fast enough, but I was glad that he hadn't. I wasn't sure that he couldn't take anything else happening to him.

Thank God that Latrel was okay. He suffered minor injuries, while Lyric and Tyese's dumb asses were dead. They wasn't wearing a seatbelt and after the car had clipped Latrel, Lyric lost control and ran into a brick wall. I should've known that Tyese was up to something when she popped up that day though. Deep down, I knew just like Lyric, she didn't like me either. It was sad because I had always been so nice to them girls, but for whatever reason, they just never wanted to see me doing good. It was all good because here I was, still standing and still strong and finally getting married to the man of my dreams. Although we were already husband and wife, this was what I had wanted and Ahmeen had made sure to deliver.

The music started playing, and I took in a deep breath, grabbed the bouquet of flowers, and finally headed out of the bridal dressing room. My nerves were so bad and everything under this beautiful ass dress was shaking, not to mention it was hugging damn near every part of my body.

We were getting married at a place called The Atlanta Event Center at Opera. It was huge as hell and fit the 400 people we had on our guestlist. Mostly all of Ahmeen's people. You know whenever he did something, he always felt like he had to bring the city out. All I wanted was for my family to be here, but the only person that I knew for certain would be here was Chuck. He was the only one that didn't trip too much with me about my relationship with Ahmeen. He didn't like it, but he was still supportive.

Soon as I got ready to round the corner that led down the aisle that I would take to meet Ahmeen, I took in a deep breath before letting it all out again. All I wanted was to not fall and bust my ass in front of all these people. Ahmeen's father had agreed to walk me down the aisle since mine had refused to answer the few times I had reached out to him. He and I had grown a close relationship over time being I hung out at his house so much when me and Ahmeen had split up.

"You ready, beautiful?"

I looked up expecting to see Mr. Shakur, but when my eyes landed on my father, my heart dropped. He was wearing an all-black tuxedo with a red tie underneath the jacket. My lips trembled as I did my best to keep from crying, but I couldn't. This was probably something that I had dreamed of more than my dream wedding. My father walking me down the aisle and giving his blessing would mean the world to me.

"Stop crying. You're messing up my make-up?"

"What...oh, my God! What are you doing here? I called you. I left messages..."

"And I wasn't ready to accept it, but I had long talk with Ahmeen and he and I came to an understanding. He let me know how much it would mean for me to be here for you, and I couldn't do nothing but respect that. Plus, you know you've always been my baby girl. I would beat myself up if I missed the opportunity to do this," he told me, and I patted at the tears that were falling.

"Daddy, thank you so much. You just don't know," I cried, unable to stop my emotions. They were all over the place, but this was nothing, but pure joy, so I let it be. "If only Maino was here, man..."

"If only Maino was here, what?"

My entire body shook and I refused to even turn around. At this point, my ass was either dreaming or I was dead. Maybe that was why nothing seemed to be going right for me. Before this day, I had dreams about all the shit that could go wrong and all of it did. Maybe this was still a dream.

"Oka...somebody wake me up," I said, and my father chuckled.

"You not dreaming baby girl," he told me and slowly, I turned around.

"Sup, baby girl," Maino said and I broke down crying harder than I ever had in my life.

I knew I was a whole mess at this point, but I didn't even care. I didn't know what was happening, how it was happening, but I was so glad that it was. My heart was beating so fast from the excitement and confusion that I felt like I was going to pass out. When I was able to get myself together, I wrapped my hands around my brother and held onto him for dear life.

"Oh, my God, what happened?" I asked him.

"Ahmeen was supposed to kill me, but he couldn't. He told me that he got caught up in my mess and of course how you had got caught up in it. Either way, he said that you would never understand and never forgive him. We ended up working something out and he helped me fake my death so that the fuckin' cartel would leave both of us alone. I know you got my flowers that I sent you a few months ago," Maino said and I chuckled in disbelief.

"I cannot believe that this is happening to me right now. My father is here...my brother is here, and I'm getting ready to marry a Shakur man and you guys are okay with it, right? Maino is alive. I'm not dreaming. This is really...this is really...." I couldn't even get it out before I started crying again.

"Yea it's happening baby girl. And nah, your pops and your brother about to walk you down the aisle. Got me fucked up if you thought I was about to miss this," Maino said as he and my father both took one of my arms into theirs.

The music began to play again, and everyone rose to their feet watching us. All the hell and bullshit I had put Ahmeen through and it was all for nothing. He always said that anything he do, he always does with me in mind. It was like as I made my way down the aisle to him, I remembered the exact words he'd said to me when he dropped on one knee and proposed to me.

I know I fucked up, but I said that if you gave me another chance, I was going to prove to you how much you meant to me. I ain't about games ma. Since I was a young nigga, I always said that when I met my queen, she would know exactly what it was like to be with a king. I would never make her doubt herself. Never make her feel like she wasn't number one in my life, never make her think she couldn't trust the nigga that said he loved her. I had broken that promise to myself and not only did I fuck up your trust, but I hurt you and I recognize that and never want to see you that way ever again. I didn't know what it was back then, but when you pulled up drunk, toting a pistol in the hood, I knew me and you was destined for something great.

Today as I prepared to stand before God and marry Ahmeen, I could truly say that I felt like I was his queen and he was my king. I felt like he had stood by what he had said and always put me first. He put everything that he stood on to the side, and for me, he got my father here, and protected my brother. He did what a real man would do. Because of him, I was the proudest woman in the world right now. Because of him, the King family and the Shakur family were one. Who would ever thought that Little Miss Poetic King would be the force that caused The Real Dopeboyz of Atlanta to stop competing and come together as a team.

The End.

SUBMIT/SUBSCRIBE

Text Shanbooks to 22828 to stay up to date with new releases, sneak peeks, contest, and more...

Shan Presents is currently accepting submissions in Urban Fiction, African American Romance, AA Criminal Romance, and Street Lit, Women's/Contemporary Fiction...

If you have a finished manuscript that you would like to send for consideration, please send the following to submissions@shanpresents.com
1)Contact information
2)Synopsis
3)First 3 chapters in a Word DOC
If Shan Presents has any interest in your work, the full novel will be requested.